KRISTA'S DEEDS

GEMMA JACKSON

POOLBEG

This book is a work of fiction. The names, characters, places, businesses, organisations and incidents portrayed in it are either the product of the author's imagination or are used fictitiously. Any resemblance to actual persons, living or dead, events or locales is entirely coincidental.

Published 2022
by Poolbeg Press Ltd.
123 Grange Hill, Baldoyle,
Dublin 13, Ireland
Email: poolbeg@poolbeg.com

© Gemma Jackson 2022

The moral right of the author has been asserted.

© Poolbeg Press Ltd. 2022, copyright for editing, typesetting, layout, design, ebook

A catalogue record for this book is available from the British Library.

ISBN 978178199-473-3

All rights reserved. No part of this publication may be reproduced or transmitted in any form or by any means, electronic or mechanical, including photography, recording, or any information storage or retrieval system, without permission in writing from the publisher. The book is sold subject to the condition that it shall not, by way of trade or otherwise, be lent, resold or otherwise circulated without the publisher's prior consent in any form of binding or cover other than that in which it is published and without a similar condition, including this condition, being imposed on the subsequent purchaser.

www.poolbeg.com

Also by Gemma Jackson

Through Streets Broad and Narrow
Ha'penny Chance
The Ha'penny Place
Ha'penny Schemes
Impossible Dream
Dare to Dream
Her Revolution

THE *KRISTA* SERIES OF NOVELLAS

Krista's Escape
Krista's Journey
Krista's Choice
Krista's Chance
Krista's Dilemma
Krista's Doubt
Krista's Duty
Krista's Deeds

Published by Poolbeg

Foreword

Dear Reader,

Welcome back. I am having so much fun writing and researching Krista's war.

In this novella I make passing reference to the Sadler's Wells Ballet Company thinking of travelling to Holland. They did, in fact, make that journey and escaped Hitler's invading army by the skin of their teeth. They hid in the locked hold of a cargo vessel.

When I read stuff like that I shake my head and wonder how they could have been so blind to what was going on around them. You read about visiting actors and musicians being forced into concentration camps. I have read the account of a Wren who was working for a high-ranking German officer as nanny to the family when war was declared. You have to wonder what they were all thinking of, to be in Germany or indeed any part of mainland Europe in the first place. It beggars belief. But then hindsight is a wonderful thing.

Then I realise I am being a hypocrite. I was in Iran when the troubles broke out between the Shah and the Ayatollah. I saw the unrest yet blithely planned my wedding! It still strikes me as unbelievable and I lived it.

I was a war bride! The restaurant catering my wedding breakfast was bombed the night before my wedding. I had to hide on the floor of the car taking me to the church, as to be seen celebrating would not be well received. My parents had travelled to Iran for goodness' sake! What was I thinking of, putting them in danger?

I walked down the aisle of the church wondering how I was going to feed my guests. For those of you who want to know – I bought a whole roasted pig and sheets of Iranian bread – *nouna barberi* – delicious stuff. We stood on the balcony of my apartment eating pork sandwiches, drinking champagne and watched the fires burning below us. It is a good thing that the young think they are indestructible.

To get my parents out of Iran, since we spoke the language, my American husband accompanied my mother, and I accompanied my father. We battled at the Tehran airport between scenes of terror. My husband managed to get himself and my mother on one of the last flights to London on that day. My father and I were left behind.

My husband spent the first night of our honeymoon in London with my mother. I was in Tehran around the pool with my father. I love my dad – but really? Dad told me I would look back and laugh about the situation someday. I am still waiting to laugh. Then he said to look on the bright side. It was the first honeymoon my mother had ever had. *Daaadd!*

So, you see, I can't truthfully write or even say people

were blind and silly to ignore the troubles in Europe. I wouldn't have a leg to stand on.

I hope you enjoy this book as much as I enjoyed writing it.

Gemma

Chapter 1

**1st September 1939
The Kent Coast
England**

"*Krista!*" A hoarse whisper and a moan that sounded something like pleasure carried softly on the breeze. "*Darling!*"

A figure, partially concealed by the long sea grass, dropped to the ground and began to crawl along, moving from the low tent hidden by the grass to the cliff edge.

The two young women, Krista Lestrange and Elaine Greenwood, were under the command of Rear Admiral Reginald Andrews – to be addressed as Reggie when away from the naval base – and were gathering information. They had been camped along the cliffs of Dover for several days, taking it in turns to crawl up to the very tip of the cliff to check the busy sea traffic.

Elaine and Krista spent their days lying flat on the clifftop. When they were on the clifftop together, Elaine primarily used binoculars to check and sketch the flags and insignia of each ship. In case anyone should see a reflection of the binoculars during the day, she gasped and cried out over all the beautiful sea birds she could see. Krista, with more experience of camping, was in charge of keeping them supplied with food and drink throughout the day. She was not a skilled artist so, when they were on watch together, she was usually the one in charge of the radio provided to listen in and make note of the chatter coming over the radio waves.

Elaine, having a French mother and having spent many blissfully happy family holidays in the South of France with her grandparents, adored anything French. She delighted in listening in to the French fishermen. Tonight, there were several ships out to sea, sailing majestically upon the waves. When one sailed directly into the light of the moon's path on the sea, flying flags showing it as a French merchant carrier, she had been delighted. While Krista went back to the tent to brew up a pot of tea, she had thought to amuse herself by listening in to the radio operator on board the ship. She twirled the radio dial, seeking the correct frequency, and prepared to be amused. The shock she received when she tuned in to the ship's radio waves had almost frozen her in place. Then she gasped Krista's name and had continued to make inane noises while she waited.

Krista, after dropping her tea-makings in the grass at

Elaine's hoarse call, had crawled along the flattened grass path they had worn into the earth over their days of camping. She reached the still moaning and panting Elaine. She had to bite her lips against the laughter that rose up inside her. Elaine insisted on providing "sound effects" suitable to the time of day. She said if they were trying to listen in to ships at sea using radio waves, then in her opinion the ships at sea could hear them too. So – sound effects.

Elaine passed a pair of headphones to her. The portable radio mast over their heads had been covered in wet mud to help conceal the glow of the chrome fittings. They didn't speak – sound carried far at night.

The German words coming through the headphones stifled any inclination Krista might have had to laugh. Clever, clever Reggie. This was what he had been looking for.

Krista rolled onto her back, holding the earphones pressed close to her head with one hand, the radio receiver in the other. She kicked out a foot, connecting with Elaine's shin.

The girls had spent time being trained by the navy to use radios and interpret Morse Code, in the company of women who were training as Wrens. They were unable to become Wrens themselves because each had one foreign parent, a fact which denied them the right to join any of the British services. War was coming to these lands. There were people gearing up to face the coming conflict. Hitler and his armies would not be stopped.

"*Darling!*" Elaine was frantically opening Krista's

waterproof coat. She understood what was needed. This was not the first time Krista had needed to take notes. "Let me help you unbutton!" She pulled out the notebook Krista stored down her front to keep it clean and dry. She searched through the many pockets in Krista's waterproof slacks, all the while uttering rubbish words of delight and affection, until she found pencils wrapped around with an elastic band, one of many bunches Krista stashed about her person.

Krista rolled back onto her front and with great difficulty began to take notes in shorthand of the conversation between what was obviously – by what was being said – a submarine officer and someone – not the captain – on board the ship representing itself as French.

Krista listened, her blood chilling as the two men discussed the trip they had just enjoyed to Ireland. They laughed and joked about the women and pub life they had enjoyed together. Then the tone of the conversation changed. They were worried about what the future held. One was very much of the opinion that Germany was going to rule the world, the other worried about his family and what world events could mean to them. Her pencil flew at speed over the paper, taking note of every word uttered.

It was a frightening conversation to listen to. These two men were long-time friends exchanging news about people and events familiar to them both. This was not orders being exchanged between equals but two friends bored and chatting. That made it worse somehow to Krista's ears. She scribbled frantically. Elaine had spare pencils to hand in case the lead on Krista's pencil broke, and turned the notebook pages for Krista. They remained like that, stiffly alert, until the ship on the sea — the one hiding the deadly submarine beneath it — sailed out of range of the radio.

"*We need to leave!*" Krista whispered, pulling the earphones off and passing them to Elaine.

While Elaine broke down the radio antenna, storing parts about her person, Krista stuffed her notebook and pencils down her shirt and into pockets. The two women checked the area to be sure they left nothing behind before crawling back in the direction of their camp site.

"*What's going on?*" Elaine whispered as they began to break camp.

"There was a German submarine under that ship."

They stared at one another for a moment, both sick at heart.

They packed up in silence after that. What could they say? They had experience now of making and breaking camp. It took only a matter of minutes to pack up their gear and put it on their navy-issue motorcycles which they had hidden behind the tent, wrapped in waterproof tarps and leaning against a farmer's fence to keep them as free as possible from any drifting sand.

Krista thought longingly of the campervan she had used in the past. Reggie was looking into getting a campervan for their use but the delays in decision-making within the navy and the reams of paperwork involved seemed to be never-ending. In the meantime, they would use a tent and make the best of it.

They left the area as they had found it. They pushed the motorcycles through the field, back in the direction of a side road they had used earlier. In the last three days they had worked their way a good distance down the coast. They wouldn't reach Dover before the naval offices opened.

They didn't start their engines until they reached the road. Still without speaking, they mounted up and, with the bikes humming beneath them, they directed their wheels towards Dover and the castle that was being turned into a naval base of operations.

The heavens opened when they were halfway along their route, dumping sheets of cold rain down on them as they travelled along the suddenly slick roads. Being thankful it hadn't rained while they camped, they lowered their chins and carried on.

The women left their muddy motorcycles parked in an out-of-the-way space surrounding the castle. In their sand-encrusted and dripping clothing, they were escorted down the white-painted tunnels under the castle by a scowling member of the naval security force.

"I will inform Commander Tate that you are here." A sniff at the state of the two women was all the reaction the man allowed himself. He had been ordered by the guard posted at the check-in point to get these two out of sight. He'd have sent them about their business with a flea in their ear if it was up to him, but the pair – to hear the guard tell it – had demanded to see Rear Admiral Andrews, for heaven's sake! Disgraceful, he thought, to even think of coming in front of a commanding officer looking like they did. They should have been taught better manners. They could have cleaned themselves up. He led them to the office Rear Admiral Andrews used when he was in the tunnels and announced he was going to look for Commander Tate.

Krista wanted to snap that they hadn't asked for Commander Tate. They wanted and needed to see Rear Admiral Andrews, not his lackey. She shook her head, telling herself to keep quiet, and let him go. Naval regulations seemed to her to be set in stone. Tate reported to Andrews so, to the navy, you had to go through Tate before you could even think of speaking with the rear admiral – and that, as they say, was that. They would just have to suffer through another one of Tate's disapproving lectures. Commander Tate had made his feelings about women becoming involved in matters of state crystal clear. The man disapproved of the brigade Andrews was trying to form, that much was obvious by his attitude and conduct towards the first two women recruited by the rear admiral – Krista and Elaine.

"What is the meaning of this?" Commander Tate opened the door to the office where Krista and Elaine waited, without offering them the courtesy of knocking. He wasn't a tall man but held himself almost rigidly erect. He stood staring at the two women in horror. "How dare you present yourself in this disgusting fashion? I will put you both on charge!"

"We need to see Rear Admiral Andrews as soon as possible." Elaine almost sighed at his bull-headed attitude. How many times and in how many ways would they have to put up with his obstructive attitude?

"One does not order a rear admiral to appear before one." Tate looked down his nose at the women. "One waits to be summoned into the great man's presence."

"Look!" Elaine longed to kick the man. "We know how you feel about us. Rear Admiral Andrews does not feel the same way. Now, can you please get in touch with him and tell him we need to see him."

"I should have you both thrown in the brig. Look at the disgusting state of you. *You are out of uniform.*" The veins on Tate's neck stood out as he tried not to scream.

"It is my understanding that you were ordered by Rear Admiral Andrews to give us every assistance, were you not?" Krista was tired, wet, dirty and hungry. If they had to play pretty party games to get along then she would just as soon not be involved in whatever Reggie was planning. "I need to clean up before I sit down. Does the navy keep any spare clothing here?"

Foolishly, they had not stopped to put on their protective clothing when the rain began to fall. They were soaked through. She would not make that mistake again. The rain seemed to have found every opening in their attire to drip into and under.

"For proper sailors – men – not females!"

"Well, if we could borrow some of those men's clothes," Elaine stepped forward to say. "Just enough to be decent. I want to go to the tunnel NAAFI to fetch something for us to eat and drink." She knew there was no point in asking this man to arrange for any food or drink to be brought to them.

"Commander," Krista stepped close to the man, "if

you could check the toilets for me, I would appreciate it. I need to clean up and I would hate to shock some Admiral of the Fleet taking a leak." There were no toilet facilities for females – yet – in these tunnels.

"Females do not belong in the services." Tate turned to leave, his back ramrod straight, his dignity in tatters. "I will have nothing to do with this madness."

"I suppose you will just have to risk shocking an admiral!" Elaine laughed at the mental image Krista's words conjured up.

"Nothing ventured, nothing gained."

Krista left the office and was in luck. There was no one in the toilets. She quickly tended to her needs, washed her face and hands and returned to find Elaine waiting for her.

"Is there an admiral needing First Aid about?" Elaine laughed aloud at the disgusted look on Krista's face as she stood in the doorway.

"Thankfully the toilets were free of any males who could take offence at the sheer presence of a female," she said, stepping into the office and standing to one side of the door. "I feel as if I'm leaving a trail of dirt and muck with every step I take." She used the toe of one boot to take off a wellington boot, repeating the move until her feet were free of both boots. She pulled the wet material of her slacks away from her legs. It was clammy and uncomfortable. Were they expected to sit around in wet clothing because Commander bloomin' Tate couldn't be bothered finding them something dry to put on?

"I'll just visit the toilets." Elaine too wanted out of their clammy clothing. "I won't be long."

While she was away Krista removed her slacks. She was wearing navy gym shorts under the slacks – enough, she thought, to protect her modesty. Her shirt had been somewhat protected by her outer clothing except for the collar and cuffs. She draped her outer wear and slacks over a chair back and looked down at herself with a shrug. It would have to do – she had matters to attend to.

She crossed the office to a large cupboard. The storage cupboard had been pointed out to her by Rear Admiral Andrews the last time they were here. She took a typewriting machine, a ream of paper and a box of carbon paper out of the cupboard, putting everything onto the large office desk meant for Reggie's use.

She arranged the sheets of paper – carbon paper for close copies placed carefully between each page – checked carefully that each inked page of the carbon paper was facing the correct way before rolling the thick wad of papers into the typewriting machine. The navy seemed to want everything in triplicate. She opened her shorthand notebook, shaking her head at the state of the mucky pages. Taking a seat before the typewriting machine, her fingers flew across the keys as she began to type.

"What can I do to help?" Elaine had returned from the toilets and now stood inside the office and to one side of the door. Seeing Krista's gear draped over a chair, she began to follow her example. The gym shorts and shirt she wore were decent – just. The Wren uniform they had been issued for use on formal occasions would never have stood up to the abuse they had submitted their clothing to in the last few days.

"I am doing the first copy of the conversation I heard in German, just to be sure I have it as I heard it." Krista's fingers continued to fly across the keys as she spoke. "When I have that done I will translate and type in English."

"Can I do anything?" Elaine hated standing around.

"Try to get in touch with Reggie on that phone there." Krista never stopped typing. "While we are waiting for the great man to appear, perhaps you could make a clearer copy of those flags and insignia you spotted on the ships as they sailed past our varied locations."

"Good idea." Elaine went to the black phone sitting on the desk to one side of the typewriting machine. She mentally crossed her fingers when she picked up the hand piece. When the operator spoke, she asked to be connected to Rear Admiral Andrews as a matter of urgency. No one was more surprised than Elaine when she was put straight through to Reggie. She spoke briefly, listened for a moment then hung up the phone.

"He is in the castle." Elaine watched Krista pull the thickly packed pages out of the typewriter and begin to make another package to put in the machine.

"If we had thought of it we could have thrown ourselves on Reggie's mercy and begged for something to eat and drink." Krista continued to type. "We never did get that pot of tea I was planning to make."

"You know," Elaine smiled, "I'm sorry I didn't think of that."

She pulled an office chair closer to where Krista was

working and with her notepad in hand, leaning on the desk, began making clearer copies of the flags that she had seen flying on the many ships she'd observed in the channel between France and England. She began with the so-called French merchant ship. When she had finished she settled down to wait, hoping she didn't fall asleep. She'd discovered she didn't like sleeping out of doors. The sounds of the night were frightening when all you had between you and the creatures that roamed was a thin piece of waxed canvas.

"What have you two been up to that has this place in an uproar?" Reggie hadn't even stepped inside the office when he started speaking. "Dear Lord!" He slammed the door at his back, closing his eyes briefly when he caught sight of the two half-naked women waiting in his office. "I sincerely hope you did not present yourselves like that to the guard on the gate?"

"We were wearing soaking wet clothes which we have since removed," Elaine said when Krista didn't even look up. "We did ask Commander Tate to supply something to cover us but he declined. We were forced to adapt." She didn't want to get the commander into trouble but the man needed to relax and offer help, not lecture and censor all the time.

"Green saw a ship," Krista said, ignoring the chatter. She was taking paper out of the machine and preparing more. "Tell him, Green." Without even thinking about it, she used the nickname Elaine Greenwood had been given while they trained with the Wrens. It would appear that no-one was addressed by their familiar name once they had passed through training. Krista herself had earned the nickname Strange. It didn't bother her – it was a direct translation of the name she had chosen for herself when she first arrived in England from France – Lestrange.

"I saw a vessel flying French flags at these co-ordinates." Elaine flipped through her notebook for the relevant numbers. "These flags were being flown." She waited for Reggie to cross the room and examine the design. When he stood at her shoulder and nodded, she turned the page. She showed him more of the insignia that had been on display. "It looked like a merchant ship. We had the antenna up and I was on listening duty. I thought to entertain myself by trying to listen in to the radio operator on the French vessel." She offered no apology. That was what they were there for.

"It would appear he had something interesting to say?" Reggie prompted.

"He might have done," Elaine answered. "I was so shocked to hear German being spoken that I shouted for Krista to take over." She stared into the rear admiral's eyes.

"Green signalled to me." Krista pulled the last sheet of paper out of the machine with a sigh of relief. She would have to proof-read them but at least she got it all down while it was fresh in her memory. "I wrote down everything I heard. I think Green must have thought she was turning sheet music for the piano at one point, but I got it all written down." She leaned her arms on top of the typewriting machine and sighed deeply. The rear admiral knew how to listen. "The words exchanged were not – in my uneducated opinion – very important. What is important is that the French ship – if it is indeed French – was providing deep cover for a German submarine sailing under it." She began to remove the carbon from between the pages of her notes.

"Give." Reggie held out his hand.

"The conversation," Krista said as the rear admiral ran his eyes over the words typed in English, "was between two friends. Two bored friends if I am any judge. One on the submarine and one on the decoy ship."

"And you were able to hear all of this clearly, using the equipment I provided." Reggie was more than excited. This could change everything. These women had surpassed his expectations.

"I had to fiddle with the radio dial a little to find the correct frequency for the French vessel," Elaine said. "The Channel is very busy as you know."

"But you succeeded!" Reggie was elated. They had found the needle in the haystack.

"It was an interesting few days," Krista said somewhat simplistically. "However, there is a matter we need to discuss. We arrived at Dover Castle, sure we had important information. We approached security as we were instructed and were almost turned away. It was only the mention of your name that got us into these tunnels and marched to this office under guard. If the information we held had been vital and time-sensitive – you would have missed it." She stared at the rear admiral.

"Indeed." Reggie, very much the rear admiral, glared

back, one eyebrow raised at her impertinence towards a superior officer.

"That is not a very efficient system, Reggie. We have no standing in the community here. Commander Tate refused to contact you on our behalf. We had to do it ourselves. He refused to even check out the toilets in case they were occupied so we could wash the muck and mud off our hands and faces. If that is the standard of liaison officer you intend to employ, I am not impressed. We are tired, wet and hungry and these bloody sailors – not for the first time – haven't even had the decency to *offer us a cup of tea!*"

"My sentiments exactly," Elaine said.

"That, ladies, will not do at all."

Chapter 2

2nd of September, 1939
Dover
Kent

"Look at the state of the pair of you!"

Marie Fagin, the woman whose cottage the navy rented for the use of Krista and Elaine, was standing in their garden.

Marie lived with her family in the cottage to one side of the rented property, her son and his family lived on the other side. She stood now, her hands on her hips, shaking her head at the muddy appearance of the two women. She'd been hanging out a load of sheets and towels when they opened the gate in the garden wall.

"You can just stand there till I run in and get you two something to put on you. You're not walking that muck over my clean floors."

"We are welcome everywhere we go; it seems." Elaine pushed her motorcycle towards the shed that served as a garage.

"Wait a minute." Krista put her motorcycle on its stand. She walked through the cleared path to the standing tap in the garden. She attached the hose old Dobbins, a near neighbour and the man who spent his days tending the land around their cottage, had left lying around. "I'll hose you and your motorcycle down." She turned on the tap and, with water spurting, turned to Elaine. "Then you can do me."

By the time the two women had the motorcycles and themselves hosed off, Mrs Fagin was back with the dressing gowns she'd taken from the back of the girls' bedroom door over her arm. She ordered them into the shed to remove their wet clothes.

"Does it sometimes feel like the world and its mother can order us around?" Elaine asked while kicking free of her wellington boots.

"Getting out of all of these clothes is an order I don't mind obeying." Krista was free of her boots and shoving her trousers down her bare legs.

"Just throw them clothes out onto the grass." Marie hurried into the shed with the two dressing gowns. "I'll hang them on the line to drip dry. I'm going to put the kettle on. I'll have to run next door to get the makings for a meal. I couldn't leave food lying about cos I didn't know when you'd be back. I'll only be a minute."

"I'm so tired even my teeth are sleepy." Elaine

shimmied out of the last of her clothes and wrapped her dressing gown around her naked body. She wanted to collapse onto her bed and sleep for a week.

"I want something to eat and drink that is hot and I haven't prepared myself over hot coals." Krista's arms and legs felt like they weighed a ton as she struggled to remove the last of her wet clothes.

"You did a great job keeping us fed using an open fire, I must say." Elaine helped Krista into her dressing gown.

The two women kicked their dirty clothes out of the shed and onto the grass before running into the cottage. They didn't even spare a glance for their surroundings as they ran for the kitchen. Steam began to issue from the spout of the kettle Marie must have put on the range to boil.

"The two of you have a load of post out in the hall." Marie came into the kitchen with a wrapped package and a canvas carrier bag. "It has been following the pair of you all over the place from the looks of the envelopes. I left it on the hall table where you could see it when you came in. You must have had your eyes closed when you came in because it's still there if you want it."

The two women, tiredness forgotten, jumped to their feet and hurried into the hall. They had not received any post since leaving London to travel to Portsmouth months ago.

"That Reggie is a fast worker." Krista stared at the gleaming black Bakelite phone sitting on the hall table. He had made mention of putting a telephone in the cottage and here it stood. He must have pulled some strings to get it put in so quickly. She picked up the handset. The line was open. She only needed to tap on the connection under the handset to alert the telephone operator of her need for a line. She replaced the receiver. "I don't know who is going to answer that if we are out of the cottage so much of the time."

"I really don't know if I am more hungry than tired." Elaine spared a brief glance for the telephone. She was busy riffling through the white envelopes with her name on the front that she'd lifted from the hall table. She examined the return addresses on the envelopes carefully, thrilled to have news from home at last. "From the sheer number of naval rubber stamps on these envelopes it looks like this post has been all over England before reaching us. Still, we mustn't complain. We have them now. I think I will read these later. In comfort. Just at this moment I don't think I could take in any news."

The sizzle of grease and the smell of bacon came from the kitchen.

"I sent out letters with my service number and the naval services post-office-box number we'd been given." Krista too was examining her own share of the white envelopes. "I was beginning to think I had made an error in passing along the postage instructions." She held the envelopes to her chest, thrilled to be receiving post. There wasn't a letter, however, from Philippe Dumas, the man she had been raised to believe was her brother. She had seen Philippe briefly when stationed in Portsmouth where she introduced him to her friend Perry. Peregrine Fotheringham-Carter was at the time seeking people with multiple language skills. Philippe spoke several languages fluently. She hoped the two men were still together. She worried about Philippe and wondered where he was and what he was doing.

"Let's have something to eat." Elaine turned towards the kitchen, the post clutched in her hand.

"I am so hungry." Krista followed along, yawning.

"It has been all go around here since you two left." Marie put plates of bacon, egg and baked beans in front of the women.

"We were only gone a few days." Krista picked up her cutlery, ready to dig in to the delicious aromatic mound of food.

"It felt like a week, I can tell you." Mrs. Fagin set cups of tea and buttered toast on the table. "What with your one Gerda acting as if her head had been chopped off, screaming and crying she was. Weeping and wailing fit to deafen a body. She wanted my Ronny to put his arms around her, if you can believe her cheek. I soon put a stop to that – and him a married man." She put an extra cup of tea on the table and sat down.

"So, Gerda has really left," Krista said. She and Elaine exchanged glances but didn't comment further.

Gerda Mueller had been a member of their group when they first moved into the cottage. She had been difficult to live with, constantly complaining and imagining slights against her from everyone around her. It had made the living situation here at the cottage very distasteful. She had carried that attitude to work with her. Reggie had told them she was about to be dishonourably discharged. It would appear that had taken place while they were away – thankfully.

"She was almost carried out of here, kicking and screaming." Marie tutted in disgust at the memory of the younger woman's behaviour. She looked at the unopened envelopes by each plate, wanting to know what was in all of them letters – but first, well, she had news of her own to share. "I'm glad of a cup of tea, I can tell you. If that one Gerda wasn't enough for me nerves to handle – the men from the GPO came stomping around the place without a by-your-leave. They told me they were putting up a telephone pole right there in the road with wires and whatnot coming out of the sky. Then if you wouldn't be minding they put a telephone in – a rush order, they tell me. Did I know they were putting a telephone in this cottage?" She slapped the table top, almost upsetting the cups. "No, I did not. It would have been polite to ask me, don't you think?"

"A telephone in the cottage was mentioned." Krista cut a finger of toast to dip in her egg yolk. "We didn't think it could be done this fast or we would have mentioned it to you. I gave no thought to having an actual telephone pole put outside the cottage." Clever, clever, Reggie! The pole would no doubt have additional wires connected in case they ever needed to use the radios from the cottage. He was certainly preparing for England to be invaded! The very thought sent shivers down her spine.

"Quite a feather in your cap though, isn't it, Mrs Fagin?" Elaine glanced at Krista quickly and away. They couldn't discuss the telephone pole in front of Mrs Fagin. She used a piece of toast to capture the sauce on her plate. "The first telephone on the road – and in a cottage you own – the neighbours must be jealous."

"Well, there is that, I suppose." Marie had let a few of the neighbours into the cottage to have a look at the thing when it was put in. She hadn't left them on their own in the cottage, mind. She'd stood over them to see they behaved themselves.

Krista could almost feel her eyes closing.

"I had them put it on the hall stand. I hope that was alright. They asked my opinion but I've never had a telephone before." Marie shook her head. "So, I had them put it where it made the most sense to me."

"That's fine, Mrs Fagin." Elaine said. "That is just the right place for it." She looked at Krista. "We'll have to put a money box by the telephone, I suppose."

"Why would we do something like that?" Krista asked.

"Mama started it in our house. We were the first house on our street to have a telephone installed." Elaine stood to fetch more tea for all of them. "It was customary in her village in France, Mama said. She told us the telephone was very useful for everyone. They could call a taxi or a doctor in an emergency. Sometimes Mama would take messages for the neighbours. We eventually had to set times when it was convenient for us. We had telephone calls coming in for the neighbours from America, Canada and even Australia at the most inconvenient of times."

"In the name of God!" Marie stared. She'd never heard of such a thing. "There will be none of that here.

That I can tell you!"

"Perhaps we should put you in charge of the telephone use, Mrs Fagin." Krista leaned back to allow Elaine to pour tea for her.

"What do you mean?" Marie watched Elaine pour her tea, her mind whirling.

"Well, you have the key to the cottage and you are a woman who knows everyone on this road. It makes sense that people would come to you to ask to use the telephone. We won't always be here." Krista had no interest in jumping to it every time the neighbours wanted to use the telephone.

"We will discuss all of that when you two wake up." Marie quite fancied herself as the one in charge of the telephone. That would put some people's noses out. That Elsie Chilvers for one. "You two are about to fall asleep where you sit. Away to bed with the pair of you! I'll tidy up here."

The two women almost crawled up the stairs to bed. They each needed a bath but that could wait until they woke up. The very thought of filling large pots with water, waiting for them to boil and carrying them up the stairs to the bathroom was exhausting.

Within minutes they were both under the covers and fast asleep.

"*Wakey, wakey!*" The shout carried through the cottage, followed by the sound of feet stamping up the stairs. "*You girls need to wake up now!*" Marie Fagin shouted. "*If you sleep any longer you'll never be able to sleep tonight!*"

The upstairs of the cottage was unusual in that all three bedrooms were reached through one doorway off the landing. The girls thought the upstairs had at one time been one large bedroom.

"*Mrs Fagin ... what time is it?*" Krista called from her bedroom overlooking the front garden. She hadn't pulled the curtains closed before collapsing into bed. The winter light coming into the room from outside gave no hint as to the time of day.

"Time you two were up and about!" Marie put her head through the door.

"I feel as if someone has beaten me with a cricket bat." Elaine groaned from her bedroom that looked out onto the back garden.

The middle room stood empty. They had checked. Gerda had really left. She had taken all of her belongings with her.

"I've pots of water on a low heat on the stove," Marie said. "I thought you two might like to clean yourselves up. You looked a right sight when you came home." She rapped her knuckles against the wooden door. She could see into each bedroom from where she stood. "*Let's be having you – rise and shine!*"

"Coming!" Krista yawned and threw the bedclothes back. "A bath sounds wonderful."

"I'll put the kettle on," Marie said. "Elaine, you need to move yourself." She rattled down the steep wooden stairs.

"I'm not getting dressed." Krista shuffled into the space that opened between the rooms. "I don't care if the King himself comes to call." She stretched and yawned.

* * *

"I don't feel as if I've had any rest." Elaine was curled into one of the stuffed chairs pulled to one side of the fire in the cottage living room, her body relaxed after the long hot bath she'd enjoyed. Open envelopes lay on the rag rug that stretched in front of the hearth. She wore a nightdress under her dressing gown, a towel wrapped around her wet hair.

"We can go to bed early tonight." Krista, similarly attired, wasn't really paying attention. She sat in her own comfortable chair, examining one of her envelopes. "Look," she leaned forward from her place across the hearth, "this letter reached Portsmouth when we were there." She pointed to the date-marked rubber stamp on the front of the envelope. "Is it really possible that, on top of everything else the sailors subjected us to at the Portsmouth naval base, they also held back our post – could anyone be so mean-spirited?"

"I'm sad to say that nothing would surprise me." Elaine took the envelope from Krista's hand. She hadn't thought to check the rubber stamps on the front of her own envelopes. "The men put a lot of time and effort into showing us our presence was resented."

"It could have been worse." Krista took her letter back. The sailors had shouted, tripped, nudged and generally made a nuisance of themselves while the men in command had turned a blind eye. It hadn't been easy to ignore them but after the abuse Krista had observed on the streets of Metz before she fled – well – you could survive what the sailors had put them through.

"I don't see how." Elaine still got angry when she thought about their treatment at the hand of the sailors on the Portsmouth base. That wasn't the navy service her father – a captain in the King's Navy – had told her about. "Though the men here in Dover haven't been helpful or welcoming."

"Oh, let's not talk about those hard-headed men." Krista rearranged her long legs, pulling the skirt of her dressing gown close. "We will meet that attitude everywhere we go. All we can do is put our heads down and get on with our work."

"I suppose," Elaine sighed. "I did want to come out swinging a cricket bat at times though."

"You are bloodthirsty!" Krista laughed. "Tell me instead about your letters. Did you get news from home?"

"I did!" She almost squealed her pleasure. "Papa is away at sea."

"I don't know how the women who are married to sailors manage. They are almost always alone. Lia –"

"Is that the woman you used to work for?"

"Yes, Lia Caulfield whose husband, like your father, is a captain in the navy. She was so kind to me, treated me like family." Krista laughed and took two large sheets of creased paper from the stack to the side of her chair. "Look," she held the pages across the hearth, "the boys sent me these drawings. They tell me they are works of art."

"Well, of course they are." Elaine took the pages with a smile. She turned them around, trying to judge which was top and which was bottom. It didn't really matter – it was the thought that counted. "These are the boys you looked after?"

"Twins, little imps of mischief." Krista didn't want to speak of her time with the Caulfield family. Not here and now. Time enough for that. She bit her lip, staring at Elaine. "I noticed one of your letters made you frown." She took the twins' artwork back. "You don't have to tell me what worries you if you don't wish." She shrugged. "I just thought it a strange reaction to news from home."

"That wasn't news from home." Elaine settled in to share her worries. "It was a letter from my friend Daffy. I don't know if I have ever told you of my wild and wonderful friend Lady Delphina Camellia and a great many more very important-sounding names which she detests. She insists on being called Daffy."

"Yes, you have shared stories about Daffy. I don't think you mentioned she was titled."

"Daffy has no time for all that nonsense." Elaine sighed, thinking of her dear friend. "We talked for years of travelling to Paris to work. I dreamed of working for one of their many fashion magazines. My father put his foot down and refused to let me even think about travelling to live and work in Paris. Not at this time, he kept saying. I'm afraid I was not a very good daughter as we argued fiercely... Daffy worked so hard to become fluent in French – she used her connections to secure a place with a famous fashion house. She is in Paris even as we speak."

"My God!" Krista slapped a hand to her mouth, her eyes like blue saucers of fear.

"Daffy loves Paris." Elaine shook the letter she'd picked up. "She refuses to even think about leaving."

27

Chapter 3

3rd of September, 1939

"We should have asked Reggie what he wanted us to do with the third motorcycle." The motorcycle had been assigned to Gerda but the woman mostly ignored it, preferring the bus. Krista, wearing the navy-blue zip-closed overalls she'd purchased to wear while working on the motorcycle, her hair covered by a scarf knotted in the turban fashion that was becoming so popular, was examining the motorcycle engines.

It was early the following day and both young women were feeling much better after the day they had spent lazing about the cottage.

"There is a lot we need to ask Reggie if you want my

opinion." Elaine, dressed in a similar fashion, was polishing the bike frames.

"Is it me or is the cottage happier without Gerda scowling around the place?" Krista said to change the subject. It wasn't safe to discuss such things out in the garden. If they could listen in to ships at sea who knew what else was possible? "Will I sound like a terrible person if I tell you I am going to buy a cafetière and coffee now that she has left us?"

"I understand completely. It is one thing to share but Gerda simply took and she did like her coffee, always complaining bitterly because the cottage had none."

"I loved Mrs Fagin's reaction every time Gerda demanded something for her comfort." Krista tightened a nut carefully.

"That woman is a treasure. She certainly knew how to handle Gerda." Elaine felt rather guilty about being so relieved not to have Gerda to face daily. The woman had loved to complain. She had also been rather free with taking anything she fancied from both Krista's and her belongings. They had fought with her over her taking ways but to no avail. At least now their belongings should be safe. They had been limited in what they could bring with them from the very first day of training. What could they have that was so different to anything Gerda might have?

"She handled Gerda far better than you or I." Krista continued to brush mud off the cables of the bike she was working on. "By the way, Gerda was nice enough to return the shampoo I've been searching for – of course the bottle is practically empty."

"*Girls, girls!*" Marie was shouting from her adjacent cottage.

"She's probably going to tell us off for working on the Sabbath." Elaine cringed slightly. Her mama would not be pleased to see her daughter outdoors looking as she did on the Lord's Day.

"Did you not hear me shouting?" Marie was at the gate. "Turn on your wireless quickly! It's happening! The BBC promised news at eleven – Mr Chamberlin is going to speak – get in quick and turn on your wireless or you'll miss it!"

There was no need to tell them what 'it' was. War. Hadn't the nation been gearing up for it?

Krista checked her watch and jumped to her feet. "You run in and turn the wireless on. We have time. I'll put the motorcycles back together and tidy up here."

"I'll put the kettle on while I'm at it." Elaine took off at a run, glad the wireless was in the kitchen. "*Thanks, Mrs Fagin!*" she shouted to the back of their neighbour.

The woman didn't respond verbally, just waved her arm over her head. She had to get indoors, not all of the neighbours had wireless sets. They'd want to come into her place to listen, she had no doubt.

The two women sat on kitchen chairs, cups of tea on the table in front of them. They didn't speak, all of their attention focused on the wireless and what it might reveal. It was tuned to the BBC. They waited – as every home in the nation was doing – waited to see what the future held for their country.

The announcement when it came was chilling. They

had been expecting it. You would have had to be blind and deaf not to notice the preparations being made, but still they had hoped and prayed all the sabre-rattling might come to nothing. Too late now. Britain was at war with Germany. The date, the 3rd of September 1939, would go down in history as the day World War II began for the British public. Who knew what lay ahead for all of them?

The telephone in the hall rang for the very first time. They both jumped, looking at each other, wondering who should answer.

"For heaven's sake!" Elaine pushed back her chair. "Someone needs to answer that thing." She went out to the hall and picked up the handset. In a clear voice she gave the area code and number printed on a sticky label attached to the telephone.

"Orders from Rear Admiral Andrews of His Majesty's Naval Service." The male voice offered no greeting. "Leading Wren Greenwood and Leading Wren Lestrange to present themselves, full dress uniform, at the Dover Castle base." The telephone call ended as abruptly as it began.

Elaine replaced the receiver and stood staring at the telephone.

"Who was it?" Krista came out to ask.

"Did you know we were Leading Wrens?" Elaine still hadn't moved.

"I beg your pardon?"

"That man," Elaine pointed at the telephone. "He said Leading Wren Greenwood and Leading Wren Lestrange are ordered to present themselves before Rear Admiral

Andrews. Full dress uniform to be worn." She stared at Krista.

"Well ... we won't find anything out until we get there. We have the uniforms even though we hardly ever wear them. Full dress uniform – that means the skirt with the jacket."

"It will be difficult to keep the skirts from blowing in the wind on the motorcycles." Elaine moved towards the stairs almost like a sleepwalker. The news from the radio and the order to appear in full uniform, plus their apparent promotion, had her head in a spin.

Krista, in camisole and knickers, stood before the open door of the wardrobe in her bedroom, staring at the uniform she had been given. It hung on a padded hanger with the hat on a shelf just above it and the highly polished brogues underneath. It almost looked like the uniform could move on its own. She took a deep breath and reached for the hanger.

"What are we going to do with our hair?" Elaine had her thick black tights and shoes on but that was all. "You know the motorcycle helmets leave it looking flat and dead. Forgive me for my vanity – Mama is French after all – but I don't want to appear in my lovely uniform, perhaps before a load of brass, with helmet hair!"

"You do a marvellous French twist – you can do it when we get there." Krista was referring to the fashion of combing the hair away from the face and twisting it into a roll at the back of the head before pinning it neatly. It was considered very glamorous. "We will each need to put a clothes brush plus a hairbrush and clips into our saddlebags on the motorcycle. We can put our uniform hats in them as well."

"We will arrive all windblown and dusty!" Elaine almost wailed.

Krista shrugged. "We will make use of the ladies' toilet in the castle before we venture down into the tunnels."

"It's a logistics nightmare. But we are women. We will arrive before Rear Admiral Andrews looking cool, calm and collected. We owe it to ourselves after the last time that man saw us and it will give that frozen Commander Tate something to think about!" She returned to her room to finish dressing.

"*Yoohoo, girls, yoohoo!*" Marie Fagin's voice carried up the stairs. "*Yoohoo, girls, did you hear the news? The neighbours are getting together to talk over things. Do you two want to come?*"

"We can't, I'm afraid, Mrs Fagin." Elaine with Krista at her heels, both looking immaculate in their full dress uniforms appeared at the top of the stairs and looked down at their landlady who was staring up at them open-mouthed from the bottom of the stairs.

"We have to report for duty." Elaine led the way down the stairs.

"Oh, girls!" Marie clapped her hands to her mouth, tears rolling down her face. "Don't you two look the bee's knees?" She didn't want to think about what these two young women – girls in her eyes – would be called upon to do. But look at them, didn't they look ready, willing and able to take on that man Hitler all on their own?

* * *

The women found a place to leave the motorcycles on the space surrounding Dover Castle. There were more vehicles than they had seen before, with sailors marching about in greater numbers. They took their hats out of the despatch bags that hung on the motorcycles and stuffed their leather jackets and helmets in.

"This place looks like a hornet's nest that's been kicked over," Elaine said softly.

Before Krista could answer a female voice from behind barked.

"Hats on your heads, Leading Wrens! Follow me, quick march!"

The two jammed their hats on their heads and quick-marched after the Wren marching away from them with her arms swinging. The woman, whose face they still hadn't seen, marched them deeper into the Castle than they had ever been before. They stopped before a door. A quick tattoo on the door by the Wren and the door swung open.

"I told you they would need to visit a lady's room." The Wren leading them stepped into a large office space. "How they expect us to travel on motorcycles or bicycles and arrive looking bandbox-fresh as if we just stepped from the cover of a magazine, I do not know."

"Mary Black!" Krista gasped when the Wren turned to face them.

In the room was a group of Wrens in shirt sleeves

and uniform skirts. They were women they had trained with in Portsmouth. How lovely to see them again!

"What on earth are you all doing here?" she asked.

"Oh, a lot of the gang are here." Andorra Prendergast smiled.

"We were ordered to report to Rear Admiral Andrews." Elaine was almost dizzy trying to see who was here and understand what was going on.

"I made use of my brother's name, I'm afraid." A smiling Violet Andrews appeared from the back of the crowd.

"Miss Andrews!" Krista stared.

"How many times and in how many ways must I remind you to call me Violet?"

"Hard to do that now you are Wren Superintendent Andrews," Andorra said with a laugh. "Poor Strange could be up on charge for insubordination."

"That will be enough of your cheek, Section Leader Prendergast." Violet was thrilled to be surrounded by women in Wren uniform – finally they were being recognised as a vital force. "This suite of offices has been set aside for use by Wrens. I will not be here on a regular basis but the offices will be the nerve centre for all Wren official business in this area. We," she gestured around the group, "are here to set up the offices and determine the work that will be carried out by Wrens here in Dover and the tunnels that run underneath the castle."

"Kick off your shoes, take off your uniforms," Andorra ordered Krista and Elaine. "There is a bathroom in there." She pointed to a door off the office. "You two need to clean up. You look like racoons with the marks from the dust that settled around your safety goggles."

"We have your braiding and insignia with us." Helen Benson took the hats off their heads. "Eugenie will brush your uniforms down. We are going to sew the braiding on your uniform jackets and hats then."

"But we cannot wear the insignia of a Wren," Krista objected. "Because of having one foreign-born parent." What was going on?

"You have been issued special badges, braiding and insignia to denote your assignment as Special Service Wrens." Violet wanted to clap her hands in delight. She had so wanted Krista to be a Wren – she would be such an asset. Now she could be, even if she still would not be recognised as a fully registered Wren.

"No time for chatter, come along now!" Eugenie clapped the two clothes brushes she held together, which reminded the girls that they had forgotten to take their own brushes from the despatch bags. "You pair are a frightful mess but, if I can make a horse's coat shine, these two uniforms shouldn't be much of a problem."

Krista allowed herself to be pulled and pushed about like a rag doll. Elaine was being treated in the same way from what she could see. They were pushed into a large bathroom with multiple stalls.

"Here!" Celine Cartwright carried a steaming kettle into the bathroom. "We have a small kitchen here in this suite for our use. We will be able to boil the kettle for tea at least. I knew you would need hot water to shift that road dust. We left scented soap on the sinks for you to use. You need to be quick, ladies."

"This beats stopping off at the public toilets and washing in cold water." Krista lathered the soap, sniffing in pleasure at the rose scent.

The two women applied themselves to removing the dust and dirt from their hands, face and necks. When they stepped back into the office, their skin rosy from the scrubbing they had subjected it to, they stopped to take in the view before them.

A group of Wrens in full dress uniform. Hats with insignia on head, jackets bedecked with blue insignia and emblems. It was quite a sight.

"You all look wonderful." Krista knew just how much this meant to Violet Andrews. The woman had fought like a Titan to reinstate her beloved Wrens. Look at her now – she was beaming.

"What you two don't know because you have been engaged in doing sterling work for the Admiralty – is that we Wrens have been busy." Violet watched her ward being pushed and pulled around. She was so pleased she could do this for Krista and Greenwood. "We have employed and trained many new Wrens and have brought Wrens down with us. Wrens who will serve here. We even have a Wrennery – an old seaside boarding house – available to us."

"That is all very well." Krista stood still while Eugenie Carpenter almost brushed her skin off through her shirt and thick black stockings. "But from what I understood, we," she gestured towards Elaine, "could not be Wrens because we had a foreign parent."

"That still holds true," Violet said. "But, you were trained with Wrens. You will be working with Wrens and we all of us consider you honorary Wrens. You wear the uniform. Your insignia will show you to be Special Service Wrens. The only two of this class – so far."

"And this urgent need to dress us in the correct uniform?" Krista looked around at the smiling women.

"We have been in Dover for the last week. We were asked to set the Wrens up here in anticipation of the announcement we heard this morning." There was a collective sigh in the room. "We heard the announcement of war." Violet pointed to the wireless in a gleaming wooden cabinet in the corner of the office. "Suddenly everyone and his brother wants to speak to the Wrens. Those telephones," she pointed to several telephones on the desks arranged around the large room, "have been bouncing around those desks with calls to requisition Wrens."

"Wren Superintendent Andrews got a bee in her bonnet." Andorra laughed, her white teeth gleaming in her animated face.

"I intend to present a strong position to the men who will work with my Wrens." Violet had been extremely angry at the treatment the women in this room experienced from the men serving here and in Portsmouth. She would not allow it to continue. Her Wrens were the best of the best in her opinion and she intended to present a strong image to the men now seeking Wren assistance.

"Lean forward until I brush your hair," Eugenie ordered Krista.

"We thought we could put our hair in French rolls." Krista objected. "You know how those helmets flatten the hair."

"You will not hide your crowning glory under your hat – not today." Eugenie insisted. "Now lean forward – who has the hairspray?"

By the time Krista and Elaine stood in front of the long mirrors in the bathroom they looked as if they had been polished. They were given no time to admire the pale-blue braiding on their sleeves or the badges on their breast and over the brim of their hats. They were ready.

"There are eleven of us in this room, Wrens." Violet felt as if her heart was going to beat out of her breast. She was so proud of everything that had been achieved. This – her Wrens going into battle – would be her crowning glory. "We will march in pairs, with me in front leading. We will march in perfect unison once we leave this office. Our route will take us through the castle and down into the tunnels. Once we leave this room we will be the personification of the Wrens. *Best foot forward, follow me, quick march!*"

They attracted a lot of attention as they marched in formation through the building and out the doors in the direction of the tunnels. Sailors jumped out of their way, whistled, yelled or pointed as they passed. They ignored it all. They had something to prove.

They didn't break formation as they moved from daylight to the electric light of the tunnel. They continued to march along, following their leader, until they reached a door deep in the tunnel. Violet didn't knock for permission to enter but opened the door wide and, leading her Wrens, stepped into a cavernous white space cut by man and nature into the cliffs over their heads. The floor of the area was occupied by men in navel uniform wearing headphones, hunched over radio receivers. She marched with her Wrens at her heels towards one of two metal staircases leading up to a natural rock formation that protruded out over the bottom floor and had been converted into a top floor with a waist-high railing running along the lip of the rock. She marched up to the admiral standing at the railing, looking down at the sailors working on the floor below.

"Admiral Sir Henry Fotheringham-Carter." Violet saluted, her Wrens following her movement in perfect synchronicity. "Wren Superintendent Andrews, sir. You wish to engage my Wrens?"

The room was eerily silent.

Rear Admiral Reginald Andrews, standing by the admiral's side, had to fight to keep a grin off his face. His sister was in her glory ready to take on all comers if he wasn't mistaken. The honour of her beloved Wrens had been impugned as far as she was concerned. He could not blame her for her attitude. He had been disgusted by the treatment Green and Strange had been subjected to. Obviously his sister intended to start as she meant to go on. He wasn't the only man in the room impressed with the appearance of the Wrens. But could they do the work?

"We have the fate of the nation in our hands, Wren Superintendent Andrews." Sir Henry returned the salute.

He had demanded the presence of the Wrens. He wanted to see for himself what they were capable of doing – he'd have no one in his service that wasn't ready to jump to and lay down their lives if necessary. He had arranged for this examination and demonstration, now he waited to see what would happen. The men in the room had been briefed.

"*Sir! There is so much chatter on the airwaves that my sailors are having difficulty sorting out individual call signals!*" a lieutenant shouted up from the floor. "Very few are using English, sir."

"What is the procedure in time of peace?" Sir Henry turned to ask the Lieutenant Commander in charge of communications who was standing, ready to jump into action, practically on his heels.

"We record any foreign conversation overheard, admiral. It is then sent for translation and if of interest passed along the chain of command."

"How do your men know which language is being spoken? They all sound the same to me," the admiral asked.

"My men are experienced, they can make a good stab at identifying each language, sir."

"Have your men shout out the language they think is being spoken." Sir Henry almost rubbed his hands together. They would see if these women were as good as Reggie and his sister claimed they were. What a coup to have them under his command!

The order was passed down the line while the Wrens looked on, studying the way the line of communication worked.

"French!" A voice called out and an arm was raised.

"Green," Violet ordered.

"Spanish!"

"Wood."

The calling out of languages, the assistance of a Wren and instant translation was impressive to watch. Violet had planned ahead. She had known the time would come when a knowledge of languages would be vital. The women chosen to lead the Wrens into this new era were women who had already fought for their place among men. They were all educated women and had chosen to learn at least one additional language to help them gain success in their chosen field. They hadn't considered this knowledge necessary in their work for the Wrens – but she knew better. It was why they were selected to lead in these early stages. She wanted to clap her hands in delight. Her planning was paying off now.

When all eight Wren leaders plus Green were engaged with one radio operator translating, Sir Henry turned to Violet Andrews.

"Impressive," he said.

"*German!*" three hands were raised.

"Strange!" Violet snapped.

Krista went to the first sailor with his hand up. She removed her hat before placing one of the earphones of the radio close to her ear. She listened for a moment before shouting for Green who she noticed was free once more, having completed her task of translating French for the sailor seated close to her. She passed the earphones over to Elaine, saying simply, "Social chatter." And moved on. She listened for a while at the second set of earphones. She took the third set and listened. "These are speaking with each other. It is important you continue to record in case they might say anything of importance but they are discussing a house of pleasure." She shrugged. "It could be code of course but it will take time to break down if that is the case."

"*Italian!*" Two sailors.

"White!" Violet ordered Mary Black to one headset. "Strange!" she ordered Krista to the second.

Violet sent Krista to translate German, French, Italian and Spanish, knowing she could do it. She might claim to have a weak knowledge of Italian and Spanish but she understood everything said in those languages – she was just slow in responding verbally. That didn't matter under these circumstances. The other women were equally as busy, flitting from one radio operator to another.

The sailors were enjoying the soft touch of a feminine hand on their shoulder. They inhaled the heady drift of some delightful floral fragrance. This little exercise was giving the sailors far more enjoyment than the Wrens who were jumping from one pair of headsets to another. It was difficult for someone who didn't speak a second or third language to understand just how difficult it was to jump from one language to another. The Wrens didn't complain but continued to demonstrate a skill most hadn't realised would be essential in their new careers.

"I want all of these Wrens under my command," Sir Henry said. "That is bloody impressive."

"You can't have them, admiral." Violet smiled demurely while the devil danced in her eyes. It felt good to deny an Admiral of the Fleet. If only once. "The Wrens here today are all Leading Wrens and engaged elsewhere. We will of course supply Wrens with language skills to man the communications centre."

"That Strange is dashed impressive." Sir Henry had met Krista before in the company of his son Perry but failed to recognise her under these circumstances. "I'd like her made available to my direct command."

"Not possible for many reasons I will not discuss here, admiral." Violet said.

"Strange is under my direct command, admiral," Reggie said. "I have more need of her many skills than you. If I might be allowed to say so, sir."

"Someone like that should be attached to headquarters," Sir Henry insisted.

Reggie knew Admiral Sir Henry Fotheringham-Carter well. He had served under the man. They could not discuss the reason Krista would not be allowed work for someone in the direct line of command of the Admiralty – not here. Besides, the man really didn't need someone of her talents – and he did.

"Admiral – " he began.

"Admiral," Violet spoke across her brother, "the Wrens who will be assigned to work in communications here will be fluent in a second language. We will endeavour to supply a Wren for all languages spoken by the combatants in this war."

"One additional language?" Sir Henry pointed to

Krista. "That young woman speaks multiple languages. That would be more efficient."

"Admiral, if I may." Reggie stepped in. He could almost see the smoke coming out of Violet's ears. "It is my understanding – speaking to the people under my command – that the use of multiple languages on a continuous basis is exhausting both mentally and physically. Far better to have people skilled in one additional European language engaged in our communications room."

"We will discuss this later." Sir Henry glared between the brother and sister. He was not a man to accept defeat. He wanted that young woman under his direct command. She was an ace in the hole as far as he was concerned.

There is nothing to discuss, Violet thought but had more sense than to say. She had deliberately shown off Krista's language skills here. It was perhaps more fluke than fate that had allowed the language skills of the other Leading Wrens to go unmentioned during training – that had been to her advantage. Today she had wanted to impress the brass and she had. The Wrens employed in this tunnel would be treated with the respect they deserved. She would see to that. Never again would her Wrens be treated with anything less than basic common decency.

Chapter 4

"Ladies!" Reginald Andrews leaned against his desk and examined the two women standing proudly at attention before him. It had been quite a sight to see the Wrens led by his sister march into the war room. He'd been proud of them. The women had been up against a great deal of prejudice and doubt but they had persevered. He looked forward to serving with them. "Ladies, my sister has seen to your insignia – about time." He had been frustrated by the delay in recognising these young women. "You will keep the uniform in pristine condition in your cabin, ready to be taken out at a moment's notice, but from here on in you will be primarily wearing your waterproofs and riding your motorcycles."

"Yes, sir!" they said together.

"Our real work will begin from this moment. I have finally been granted the special status I requested." He had been beating his head against a brick wall for months. With the declaration of war, he had finally been granted permission to instigate his plans.

Krista and Elaine waited.

"I have been impressed with the work you have carried out for me." Reggie couldn't wait to get his teeth into his long-delayed plan of action. "In future I will endeavour to have back-up available to you when travelling out to remote locations …"

"Yes, sir?" Krista prompted when he seemed to become lost in thought.

Elaine tried not to look at Krista. What was going on here?

"You will be having more overnight stays away from base that you will need to plan for." Reggie wasn't sure of the exact nature of the work in front of them but these two had proved very inventive.

"In fields, sir?" Elaine tried not to cringe.

Reggie could read the distaste on Green's face.

"I want you to put your heads together and plan a travel kit that you can take with you on your motorcycles. You might even carry a rucksack but you must be ready to camp out for days at a time. I will give you two days to get your travel pack together and then we will see what is ahead of us."

"May we ask what exactly we will be doing, sir?"

Krista asked. "It is difficult to plan for something when you have no information."

"We will be seeking out emplacements for radio towers. You two have already discovered some ideal sites. We will travel up the coast using the methods that have worked for you – improving upon them when we can. When we have what we believe are optimum sites, we will mark them and move on."

"Yes, sir." Krista thought that was as clear as mud and who was this 'we' he spoke of?

"Green, something you said has been bothering me." Reggie looked at the brunette of the pair. He had heard these two women referred to as Reggie's Rashers, meaning "smashers" or beauties. It amused him. "I bring it up now because I wonder if it is something we need to discuss with Wren Superintendent Andrews."

"Yes, sir." Elaine waited.

"You said that, when you listened in to the radio operator on that French ship, you could barely understand a word he said. It was my understanding that you spoke German."

"I do, sir." Elaine's knowledge of the language had been improving with Krista's help. "However, listening to someone speak to you face to face or indeed over the wireless is one thing. Listening and trying to understand a foreign language with buzzing and crackling in your ear is quite something else. I may have panicked when I realised a ship flying French flags was transmitting in German."

"You had no difficulty, Strange?"

"It was difficult, sir," Krista said. "Green's French, as I know, is first rate. I have helped with her German and it is coming along. But, in that moment on that cliff, with my speed at notetaking, thanks to my shorthand skill – I was the better one to listen and Green knew that – she made the right decision to pass the earphones to me ... sir."

"Wood has expressed an interest in joining you two."

"Did she, sir?" Elaine looked at Krista.

"Did you know Wood spoke Spanish?" Reggie had been surprised at the language skills displayed by the women his sister had selected to lead her Wrens. She'd kept that fact close to her chest.

"Sir, we were – all of us – so intent on learning what the navy was demanding of us. Green, Mule and myself tried to find time to practise our language skills. From time to time one of the Wrens passed a remark in whichever language we were speaking but since we did not use Spanish – well, sir – how would we know?"

With the problems the women had learning the required skills, the constant worry and need to guard against what the seamen had planned. There was not a great deal of time to sit around chatting. They had simply got on with what was asked of them.

"Eugenie Carpenter – Wood." Reggie took a file off his desk. "A three-day eventer. She has to have strength, skill and a massive amount of sheer guts.

Three-day-event horse trials were among some of the toughest in the world, demanding much from both horse and rider.

"I was surprised she asked to join us but according to the notes in her file it would appear she does not do well in enclosed spaces – did you know of this?"

"No, sir," Elaine answered for both of them.

"Yes," Reggie slapped the file against his open hand. "A lot of the work the Wrens will be asked to do will be in the tunnels under the castle. Then apparently the office space set aside for the Wrens has no windows, being deep inside the castle. Wood would prefer something out in the open air. What do you two think?"

"We could use a despatch rider, sir," Krista said immediately. "Wood is fast and fearless on a motorcycle." They had trained together after all. "She has nerves of steel. If we could remain at our listening post but send someone back to keep you informed of anything we consider too delicate to send over the airwaves it might be more efficient."

"You have an extra motorcycle at your disposal. You would have no objection to Wood sharing a cabin with you two?"

"No, sir," said Krista.

"If the motorcycle runs out of petrol, sir," Elaine laughed, "Wood could grab a horse from the field and still get her message to you."

Reggie could see where having a horse-riding three-day-eventer under his command could come in useful. Although the woman was so small and delicate-looking, she should be called 'Woodchip'.

"We would be Strange Green Wood," Krista smiled. "Easy to remember, sir, in the heat of the moment."

"True." Reggie liked their attitude, respectful but not fearful. "I have been in contact with Captain Waters, Strange, as you suggested. There are talks in place with other arms of the services concerning the use of campervans. I have placed an order but at this stage it seems to be a case of 'hurry up and wait'."

"Yes, sir." Krista was disappointed.

Green tried not to groan – more time spent in a tent.

"Dismissed." Reggie had planning of his own to put in place. "You should collect Wood and take her back to your cabin with you. She will need to be a part of the planning for – what we will call – your camping trips."

"Yes, sir."

The two women left the office.

"Where do you think we'll find Eugenie?" Elaine walked alongside Krista, heading out of the tunnels. She was glad she wouldn't be one of the women working in this dark and forbidding place.

"If we head for the office set aside for the Wrens, someone else can look for her."

"Oh, learning to delegate already, Leading Wren Lestrange!" Elaine wanted to laugh out loud but was on her dignity because of her dress uniform. She couldn't let the side down.

"We need to make careful lists of what may be of use to us," Krista said as they exited the tunnels. "Although, to be honest with you, I thought Reggie's instructions were as clear as mud."

"They did leave something to be desired."

They walked through the castle towards the office suite the Wrens would use, both thinking of what might lie ahead. They were delighted to find all of the Wrens back in the office suite, hats and jackets off, mugs of tea in hand.

"Fancy some tea?" Andorra asked.

"Please, I'm gasping!" Krista said.

"Me too," Elaine added.

"*White, two more teas out here!*" Andorra shouted over her shoulder.

"Another one who is learning to delegate." Elaine nudged Krista.

"Wren Superintendent Andrews," Krista looked towards a very relaxed Violet, "we were informed that Wood wanted to join our group."

There were shouts of outrage from the women present and all heads turned to look at where Eugenie almost cringed in a corner.

"Oh, bless you, Violet!" Eugenie had explained her problem to Violet Andrews in the hopes that something could be done. She wanted to serve but the very thought of working in those tunnels or any enclosed space sent her into spasms. She looked at the other women she had grown close to in the last months. She hated to leave them but, at the same time, she could not be imprisoned between four walls.

"Here," Mary Black 'White' almost shoved two mugs of tea into Krista and Elaine's hands. "There is sugar and milk on the table there."

"What is going on?" Andorra was the one who asked the question everyone was thinking.

"Andorra," Eugenie stepped forward – she could speak for herself, "if everything goes to plan you will be training and in command of the Wrens manning the ferry boats. You will be outdoors, your feet on your beloved decks. Helen, you will be in command of the despatch riders. You will be out of the office constantly." She looked around the room and, with a shrug, continued. "They want to put me in an office – manning the phones and writing reports or some such. I cannot do it. I am sorry. I can't be inside four walls all the hours of the day. I can't breathe and when I have to go into those tunnels, I break out in a cold sweat."

"But a knowledge of Spanish is not one of the languages so desperately needed for our Special Services Wrens, is it?" Mary Black said. "I could understand if Spain was still at war within its own borders but that war has now ended."

"Wrens," Violet had allowed them to get their questions out in the open before stepping in, "I knew of Wood's difficulties. I fought to keep her with us, I can assure you."

"Wood would be ideal for teaching physical fitness," Celine Cartwright offered. "She could soon have our Wrens marching in step."

"Denied. Every duty I suggested Wood might be ideal for – the navy insists men must cover. I was at my wits' end when I remembered our specialists." Violet pointed to Krista and Elaine. "They look wonderful in our uniform. They are a credit to the service and yet they are not allowed join the Wrens proper. The uniform they wear so proudly today will be kept in their cabins. They are out and about in all weathers, wearing whatever garments will serve. Something of that nature will suit Wood far better. I asked Reggie to consider Wood. I am delighted he has given her this chance to continue to serve."

"I'm sorry if you all feel I'm letting you down." Eugenie looked around the women who had been her constant companions for the last months.

There were loud disclaimers while the women wished Wood well. They couldn't ask her to make herself ill.

"Your suitcase is at the Wrennery," Violet said.

"We can take you to collect it," Krista offered. "One of us can take you and the other your suitcase."

"We have an additional motorcycle in our shed." Elaine had wondered what was to become of Mule's motorcycle. Now she knew. "I am sure you will be able to put it to good use."

There were hurried hugs and best wishes while the address and telephone number of the cottage the three women would be using as a home base was taken down. The three women left the building, marching in formation. It was important to keep up the image the Wrens wanted to present.

"I suggest we change out of these uniforms and put the kettle on," Krista said. She took the suitcase off the back of her motorcycle and made for the cottage door. It had been a long stressful day and she just wanted to relax.

Elaine and Eugenie followed on her heels.

"I think I'd better move into the middle room upstairs," Elaine said. "If Eugenie suffers indoors, she doesn't need the only room without a window to the outdoors."

"I can move if you prefer," Krista offered.

"I don't want to cause problems." Eugenie held up one hand. "I don't need a room with a view – honestly

– I just sleep in a bedroom. My eyes are shut. So, the middle room sounds fine for me. If that changes, I promise I will tell you."

"We will try that for now." Krista was relieved. She didn't fancy moving her belongings tonight.

Krista led the way upstairs. They showed Eugenie to her room and then with deep sighs of relief began to remove their uniforms.

"It's late enough," Elaine's voice carried to all three bedrooms. "We can just wear pyjamas."

All three women were sitting in the kitchen, steaming cups of tea on the table in front of them.

"*Yoohoo, girls, yoohoo!*"

"That's our landlady, Mrs Fagin," Krista said. "We are in the kitchen, Mrs Fagin!"

Marie came into the kitchen a dish of something wonderful-smelling in her hands. "I hope you like fish pie. My Ronny brought some of his catch home to me." She put the dish on the stove top before turning. "Mercy me, there's another one!" She clapped her hands to her face.

"Mrs Fagin, this is Eugenie Carpenter – she is joining us," Krista said. "Eugenie, Mrs Fagin is our guardian angel. She supplies food, answers the telephone when we are not here, picks up our post. Arranges for someone to tend the garden. There is no end to the chores she does for us."

"Nice to meet you, Eugenie," Marie said, smiling.

"I will try not to add to your workload, Mrs Fagin," Eugenie said.

"Oh now, a little thing like you! Why, I'll hardly know you're there." Marie helped herself to a cup of tea, pulled out a kitchen chair and sat down to join them. "I wanted to tell you, I've telephoned the gasman. I put money in the box for the telephone call. Anyway, I've ordered a gas water-heater for the bathroom. You girls can't be carrying big pots of boiling water up them stairs. It's dangerous. Now, according to that wireless and some men who came knocking on all of our doors today, we have to put blackout curtains over every window – have you ever heard the like? – you girls don't need to worry about that – me and my girls will soon run them up on my sewing machine and my Ronny will hang them for all of us. It's been all go today, I can tell you."

"What did I tell you, Eugenie?" Krista smiled. "A guardian angel."

"Get away with you!" Marie wished she thought to bring in a packet of biscuits. These girls didn't look after themselves. "Now the gasman wanted to know if I wanted to put in a money meter. On account of your renting the place from me. I told him no. I can't be doing with all that. We'll use the honour system just like we do for our telephone."

"We will need to sort that out, Mrs Fagin." Krista said. "What about money for the blackout curtains? We don't want you to be out of pocket."

"Them curtains is my responsibility – as the owner of the cottage." Marie could see she wasn't going to get any gossip out of this lot. They looked exhausted. "Well, we won't solve the problems of the world sitting here. You girls should eat that pie before going to bed — and you left the motorcycles in the garden — you should put those in the shed under lock and key before you go to sleep."

"*Yes, Mrs Fagin!*" Krista and Elaine said together.

"That's the way I like things to run." Marie laughed left the kitchen and let herself out of the house.

"Guardian angel or headmistress?" Eugenie looked after the woman.

"A bit of both but she has a heart of gold and can't do enough for us," Krista said. "She really has been a blessing to us."

"Not to mention 'my Ronny'," Elaine put in.

"Her husband?" Eugenie asked.

"Her only son." Krista and Elaine laughed.

Mrs Fagin referred to 'my Ronny' so frequently that it amused the two women. They had begun to refer to the man in the same fashion — but only when alone.

"It will all seem clear as a bell in the morning," Krista said. Tomorrow when they would have to plan their future duties. Tonight, well, tonight she just wanted to sleep.

Chapter 5

December 1939
Near Cromer, Norfolk Coast, England

"Where on earth have these crazy women got to?" Peregrine Fotheringham Carter, hunched over the truck's steering wheel, squinted through the rivers of rain hitting his windscreen. The truck headlamps were next to useless in the mucky dark but he soldiered on – he had to find the women. "If I drive much further along this coast road I am going to fall off the end of the earth."

He had been searching along this coastline for what felt like days but was in fact merely hours.

Then he saw them.

"*Noooo!*" Perry could not believe what he was seeing. Were these three women demented? What were they thinking of?

He inched the truck off the road, over a grass verge and onto the wet sand, horrified by the scene the headlamps revealed.

"*Do not attempt to scale that cliff,*" he muttered under his breath, unable to believe they were still out here.

He'd been afraid the wind and rain were almost enough to blow the truck he was driving over. Yet here they were – were they insane?

Opening the driver's door, he shouted, "*Do not even think about scaling that cliff!*"

He left the truck's headlamps on and the engine running. He jumped nervously out of the truck onto the wet sand. The last thing he needed was for his weak leg to collapse under him now. He didn't take the time to put on his foul-weather gear – he had visions of the women falling to their death while he did that. He had to get them out of this weather. He bent into the wind and walked towards them.

"*Get away from there!*"

Elaine Greenwood, standing at the bottom of the cliff, her black hair covered by a fisherman's rain hat, turned her head, blinking the water out of her blue eyes, to see a man bent almost double heading in their direction and shouting though his words were lost in the wind.

"*Get away from there now!*" Perry wanted to close his eyes against the sight of Krista, a thick length of rope coiled over her shoulder, attempting to scale the monolithic rock that rose from the beach. He stood on the wet sand, put his hands around his mouth and shouted, "*Krista, get down! NOW!*"

"Who are you?" Eugenie Carpenter, her brown eyes blinking rapidly against the salt-laden moisture that blew into her face, looked smaller than ever in the concealing wrap of her foul-weather attire.

"Peregrine Fotheringham Carter — at your service." Perry didn't turn to look at the woman. He was watching Krista slowly inch her way back down the pockmarked rock. Thankfully he had arrived on the scene before she had reached any great height.

Krista reached the bottom. "Perry," she said, "what are you doing here? You're soaking wet — where is your raincoat?"

Perry stared, his mouth hanging open. Did she just ask him about his raincoat?

"Are you insane, Krista Lestrange?" He pointed wildly towards the rock and the cliff face. "Birds nest in those crevices. You need wings to get up there. What were you thinking?"

"I wanted to check out the radio reception from the top of that rock." Krista shrugged. It wasn't the first time she'd climbed up a rock face and the marks in this rock made climbing comparatively easy. She'd had the idea that perhaps the radio waves would bounce off an antenna placed on top of the rock onto the cliff face, giving a larger area of radio coverage. She had been protected from the wind by the monolithic rock but now down on the wet sand she could understand Perry's worries. Time to leave.

Eugenie and Elaine looked between the two while trying to dry off the equipment, with a cloth each had taken from her pocket, doing the best they could under the less than ideal circumstances, before stuffing the equipment inside their wet gear.

"I am ordering you ladies to stand down and follow me." He ignored her words – they didn't deserve consideration. He pointed dramatically towards the truck, its engine idling, sitting on the sand. He turned and began to march back towards it. He didn't wait to see all three drenched figures begin to follow him. "Where have you left your motorcycles?"

"In a shed down there," Krista pointed down the beach beyond the truck. "We need to get them. This wind has really picked up since we left them there. The shed didn't look very substantial." She blinked her startlingly blue eyes and blew a raspberry with her lips, trying to combat the sheets of water flying into her face.

"Come along. I want to get out of this storm even if you three twits don't."

The women ignored his comment. They knew what they were doing. These women had fought tooth and nail to carry out the duties required of them. They had been mentioned in despatches for their daring. They had mapped the southeast coast of England up into Norfolk, searching for ideal spots to erect radio-wave towers.

"Get your motorcycles while I turn the truck around. I'll follow you down the beach." Perry shook the rain from his head in disgust.

He turned the truck and followed the women, their bodies bent against the wind as they fought their way to a weather-beaten shack that didn't deserve to be called a shed.

He got down from the truck and followed them into the shed. The motorcycles and their few meagre belongings were inside and seemed to be dry. The radio and antenna they used to track radio waves were tucked inside each woman's shirt. He'd seen them put the items away with his own eyes, shaking his head at the sight. They took better care of the equipment than they did themselves.

"We need to get the motorcycles loaded into the back of the truck." Perry stood inside the shed, water dripping from him. He shook his head at the sight of the three bedraggled figures. They looked pitiful. They were far from it. What these three had achieved in the months since the declaration of England's war against Germany was nothing short of miraculous. His father Admiral Sir Henry had kept Perry and Captain Waters of the army up to date on the work of these women.

"Perry, what are you doing here?" Krista, water dripping from her, stared at the rain-soaked figure.

"Follow me. I have found a camping site out of this infernal wind. We will set up camp, get dry, only then will we talk." He led the way out to the truck and with loud grunts pushed open a sliding door. He bent into the dark interior and pulled a ramp forward, sliding it out until it reached the ground.

"Perry, what is going on?"

Elaine and Eugenie just wanted to get out of this weather. The thought of being dry and warm was all they could think about.

"Later, Krista, for heaven's sake!" Perry snapped. "If we don't get out of this rain we are all going to get pneumonia. Just push the dratted motorcycles up the ramp and into the body of the truck." He stepped up into the truck.

The three women pushed their motorcycles into the truck. Perry retracted the ramp and slammed the door closed. He lowered a string coiled against the roof and gave a quick jerk. Light suddenly illuminated the interior.

"This is amazing!" Eugenie, motorcycle in hand, simply stared.

"I've never seen anything like this ..." Elaine tried to turn her whole body around but her motorcycle stopped her.

"Perry –" Krista began.

"Ladies, I am cold, wet, tired, hungry and extremely angry. Could we keep the questions until later? Right now, you three need to push the motors down the truck to the back."

He followed them as they obeyed his instructions.

When all three motorcycles were leaning against the locked rear door of the truck, he unclipped a cleverly concealed partition from each side of the truck and pushed them into position in front of the motorcycles, effectively making a storage space for them. He pulled another length of partition from the wall, snapped legs into place creating a bench and with a wave of his hand invited the women to take a seat.

"I'm going to get us out of here." He pulled the string to turn off the overhead light but left it dangling, then walked towards the driving section of the truck. "Hold on, it won't be a long trip." He climbed into the driver's seat and without a backward glance put the truck into gear.

The women, relieved to be out of the cold and rain, sat in darkness while the truck travelled along the coast, waiting to see what would happen next. They held onto each other when the truck made a sharp turn and the engine was turned off.

"Wait until I get the generator attached to the power!" Perry shouted from the front.

The women leaned their heads against the side of the truck, content to just wait.

"Got it!" Perry's voice was coming closer. "Krista, get the light."

Krista stood up. Slowly leaning forward from the waist, she put her hands out searching for the string that Perry had left dangling from the roof. She found it and tugged, lighting the truck interior.

"I'm going to change out of these wet clothes." Perry, a rucksack over one shoulder, pulled open a section of the wall, revealing a toilet and washbasin. "You three should get out of your foul-weather gear – you can hang it to drip-dry in the toilet when I'm through." He stood outlined by the light in the toilet. "Krista, there is a mop and bucket in the kitchen. You'll need it."

"Kitchen? What kitchen?"

He stepped inside the bathroom and pulled the door closed before she could question him further.

"Elaine, help me with these boots, please." Krista sat back down on the bench and held up one leg.

"We will need to find that mop. I don't fancy standing

on a wet surface. Surely our socks at least are dry." Elaine put both hands on Krista's foot to coax the wellington boot off. "I can't feel my feet."

The three women helped each other remove the waxed gear, wincing at the water dripping off their clothing and onto the floor of the truck.

"The kitchen must be in a hidden compartment somewhere." Krista scrutinised the walls. "Do you think if I said '*Open Sesame*' I might find the openings?"

"I think you need an Aladdin for that," Eugenie said.

"And his lamp," said Elaine.

Krista started patting the walls of the truck. She cried out in relief when her fingers found a circular metal pull sitting flush against the wall. She put her fingers in the ring-pull and tugged. One part of the wall opened, to reveal a camper kitchen. A mop, bucket and brush were off to one side, attached by magnets to the wall.

When all three women were standing well away from the dripping outer garments, each in slacks, jumpers with leather patches at the elbow, woollen stockings on their feet, the toilet door opened.

"Perry, this thing is amazing," Krista said almost before he had stepped into the main body of the truck. "Where on earth did you get it?"

"Green, if you would carry the wet clothes into the toilet," Perry said, ignoring Krista. "They can drip-dry in there and the water will run out through a hole in the floor."

Elaine, with a sigh, put her wellington boots back on. She wasn't willing to get her feet wet. Without a word she began to carry out her instructions.

"Wood," Perry continued, "if you would mop the floor dry."

Under Perry's direction, the women cleared the floor and mopped it dry before assembling a foldaway square wooden table and chairs.

"Everything in this truck is designed with an eye to maximum use of the space." Perry looked around the interior like a proud parent. "Krista, come help me in the kitchen."

They entered the small kitchen.

"We have a bottled-gas cooker in this rig." Perry pointed it out to Krista. "I had one of the camp cooks prepare a stew for us. I didn't fancy trying to stop and shop for food." He flashed his dimpled smile. "I didn't want to eat cold food either." He bent to open a foot locker attached to the wall, revealing food stuffs. He took a large sealed metal container out of the locker and gave it to Krista. "I hope one loaf of bread is enough for now."

She put it on top of the container.

"I'm going to light the fire."

Perry's words had Krista's head turn so fast she almost gave herself whiplash. What fire? Where was it? She wanted to see this.

The three women stood shoulder to shoulder and watched in open-mouthed amazement when Perry revealed a hidden cast-iron freestanding fire. With practised movements, using the kindling from the storage box to one side of the fire, he soon had a flame burning. The groans of pleasure at the first touch of heat from everyone in the vehicle were almost loud enough to carry over the storm outside.

"I'll get that stew on." Krista couldn't stand here and watch Perry add fuel to the flame – much as she wanted to. She hurried into the kitchen.

Elaine set the table with the enamel mugs and bowls Perry pointed out to her. Eugenie sliced the loaf of bread into thick slices while Krista heated the thick hearty stew on the gas stove. The smell was enough to bring tears to their eyes.

Chapter 6

"Right," Krista said when they were all seated around the table, full bowls of stew before them and thick slices of bread close to hand. "You can tell us about this magical vehicle if you please, Perry, and while you are about it – without giving me the lecture I can almost see on the tip of your tongue – you can tell us what you are doing here? Do you have orders for us?"

"We will eat and listen," Elaine said before the two could get into an argument.

"I'm fighting the need to bury my nose in my bowl like a horse with a nosebag," Eugenie said, hoping they would not argue. She didn't want indigestion while eating the best meal she'd had in what seemed like ages.

Perry glared at Krista. What was the point? She wouldn't listen to him anyway. He sighed. Fighting off all of his childhood training, he spoke with his mouth full. "This truck is the first of its kind. My father, Captain Waters of the Armed Forces and Rear Admiral Andrews have had the combined forces engineers and boffins scratching their heads and burning the midnight oil to build a vehicle that will serve as a travelling base for women such as yourselves."

"It is truly astonishing. You will have to show us around." Elaine too spoke with her mouth full. "And explain to us why everything is hidden behind panels. Not that I'm complaining – it will be marvellous not to have to spend hours searching for rooms to rent at the end of the day – not to mention sleeping out under the stars." On more than one occasion a landlady had slammed the door in their faces. Close to the coast, however, they could usually find a willing landlady when they showed their naval identity card.

"I intend to show you all of the services on this truck." Perry was beginning to feel almost human again, thanks to the heat from the fire and the food in his stomach. "There will be a written exam afterwards." He laughed at the women's groans. "We need to know how well this vehicle serves your needs and what if anything you would change or add. You three are the experts after all. The first group of your kind."

"Can we put off any written exams until after we have had some sleep?" Krista begged.

"Time enough for written exams. Now – I know Krista can drive but can you two ladies?" Perry didn't think Eugenie could reach the pedals in the truck but didn't like to say so. It might hurt her feelings.

"I never learned to drive." Elaine shrugged.

"I'm willing to learn but I too have never learned to drive," Eugenie said.

"I think that is going to be a problem that needs to be discussed at a higher level." Perry had feared driving would be a problem for the women now being selected to engage in Rear Admiral Andrews' plan to travel the country and map its coastline.

The four were silent for a while, each enjoying the food.

"This stew is delicious," Eugenie was using a chunk of bread to soak up the liquid remaining in her bowl. She didn't care about exams. She'd worry about that after she'd had a night's sleep.

"I hope we're not using up all of your supplies?" Elaine had almost finished her bowl and wanted desperately to ask for another.

"Just help yourself if you want more," Perry said. "We won't stand on ceremony." He smiled when Elaine almost ran to the stew-pot keeping warm on the stove. He was glad he'd thought to have something ready to hand for when he found the women. The army chef had grumbled but, if it wasn't his hunger talking, that had been a dashed fine stew.

The four continued to eat their food in silence. The wind sent sand rattling against the truck but inside all was cosy and warm. The only noise was the movement of spoons as they enjoyed the thick stew.

"That was marvellous." Krista pushed her empty bowl from her. "I do believe I am almost thawed." She carried her bowl over to the wash basin. She'd put a kettle and a pot of water on the stove for tea and to wash the dishes. "I'll make us a pot of tea." She had seen the makings for tea while searching the cupboards.

"I'll wash the dishes." Elaine began to remove dishes from the table. "If you'll show me how. I've performed kitchen duty in my father's galley aboard our own boats. I imagine this would be something of the same." She raised a brow in query at Perry.

"It is much the same thing." Perry shrugged. "Krista can show you how."

"I'll dry," Eugenie offered, wanting to see how things were run on board this travelling home.

"I'll put away since I know where everything goes," Perry said. "I'll just add more fuel to the fire while we get organised."

With many hands to take care of the work, they were soon back sitting at the table, cups of tea in hand. There was a punctured can of carnation condensed milk sitting on the table and an opened packet of sugar cubes for anyone wanting milk and sugar in their tea.

"Perry, once again – what are you doing here?" Krista asked as she prepared a cup of tea for herself. "This truck is amazing but you didn't drive all of this way just to get our opinion."

"I've come to take you three back to Dover," Perry said.

"*What?*"

"*Why?*"

"When?"

"Ladies, I have my orders. You three are to return to Dover. I wasn't jesting when I said your opinion of this truck was needed. Also, there are people who want to speak with you. Get your opinion of the work you have carried out and what more could be achieved by groups such as yourselves."

"Well, at least we'll be travelling in style." Krista wasn't going to question orders. It would be a relief to get off the motorcycles and out of the bitter winter weather.

"Some of us may even receive leave to return home for Christmas." Perry smiled at the looks on their faces.

"They are saying this is a phoney war in the newspapers and on the wireless." Eugenie looked at Perry, wondering if he knew more than they did. "That we should all just pack up and go home."

"This is the lull before the storm." Perry searched in the pocket of his heavy worsted trousers for his cigarette case. "No one in their right mind would try to cross our channel in winter. Come the spring – look out."

"I've read in the newspapers that the children who were sent away at the first mention of war have been returned home." Elaine too watched and wondered.

Krista listened and wondered.

Perry offered his cigarettes around the table. Eugenie took one but the other two refused.

"It would seem that a lot of people believe that Hitler will leave England alone – they are fooling themselves. Everybody in England, Scotland and Wales will feel the grip of war before too long." Perry put a match to the cigarettes. "I'm not sure where Ireland stands in this but it wouldn't surprise me if they decided to remain neutral. Many European countries have already declared their neutrality."

"Much good it will do them!" Krista snapped. "Herr Hitler will no more recognise their right to choose than he honoured the peace agreement he made with England."

"I hope you are wrong, Krista," Eugenie said. "I have friends in the Sadler's Wells Ballet Company. There are talks of the company travelling to Holland in the new year." She had trained for years in ballet because of her small stature. She enjoyed it but it was horses she loved. The feeling of power and self-worth she experienced when riding and controlling a horse was priceless to her.

"I have a friend in Paris," Elaine put in. "I worry about her safety."

"I don't know what to tell you ladies." Perry puffed on his cigarette. He knew a great deal more than he was able to share. The people of Britain were being kept in the dark – newspapers and the wireless were being controlled by the government. All stories of the horrors taking place in Europe were being repressed. "All we can do is wait and see. There are people planning for the worst and praying for the best, as far as I can see. The sea will be our greatest defence."

Eugenie stared at Perry through the smoke from her cigarette. "We have been out and about with the fishermen hereabouts, Perry. You can't but hear them talk about their worries when they gather for a pot of tea in cafés or a pint in pubs. A great deal will be expected of them – we will need them to continue fishing – but with the danger of armed ships on the sea – how are they to keep their crews – often family – safe?"

"I'm no expert but of course there will be a great deal of new dangers for all men of the sea," Perry replied. "The sea will protect us – no doubt about that – but, on the other hand, we rely on supplies coming in by sea. That's a worry to one and all."

"It sounds like that storm is settling in, Perry." Krista added milk from the can to her tea. "Are we going to spend the night in here?" The heat from the fire was making her drowsy.

"Yes, the divide holding the motorcycles in place flips and with pull-out legs forms a platform. It won't be very comfortable but we'll be warm and dry. For those of us who prefer, there are hooks for hammocks. You can get a good night's sleep in a hammock, as I know."

"I'll take a hammock," Elaine said quickly, with delight. "It will be far softer than sleeping on a wooden platform although I have never tried to climb into a sleeping bag while swinging on a hammock. I suppose there is a first time for everything."

"I've never slept in a hammock," Eugenie smiled, "but I am so tired I believe I could sleep on broken bottles."

"If we are going to serve the navy then I suppose we should be able to sleep in a hammock – at least once." Krista was willing to give it a try.

"I am going to let the fire go out." Perry yawned. "It

would be too dangerous to leave it burning overnight." He stood. "Let me show you where the hammocks are stored."

Working together, they got the truck ready for the night. Four hammocks were soon swinging from hooks set securely into the truck frame.

There was a slight difficulty with decorum with Perry being a single young male but it was soon ignored. They would sleep in the clothes they wore for warmth. They were simply too tired to trouble with the proprieties.

It was early morning when the foursome began to stir.

"I'll check our camp site." Perry opened his sleeping bag and with a great deal of manoeuvring rolled out of his hammock.

"I'll get the kettle on." Krista's head appeared over the top of her sleeping bag. "Perry, is there any fuel for the fire left in the storage box?"

"I'm afraid not."

"See if there is any driftwood outside, please. A fire to warm us while we wake up would be great."

"That sounds heavenly." Elaine sighed. "Heat and a pot of tea – what more could we want?"

"Breakfast," Eugenie muttered into her sleeping bag, unwilling to face the day just yet.

Perry left them to mutter and grumble. He stepped out of the truck onto the damp packed sand. The world before him was washed clean by the storm that had raged through the night. Fishermen were already out and about checking their boats and nets for storm damage. He stretched and yawned while visually searching the beach for driftwood. There was a great deal of it to be had. He began picking up small pieces that would burn quickly, giving instant heat. They needed to get on the road. They had a long drive ahead of them.

"Krista, since you appear to have experience travelling in a home on wheels," Elaine, still in her sleeping bag, took a controlled fall out of the hammock, "we will take our orders from you." She shimmed out of the sleeping bag and stood for a moment stretching and yawning. "Would there be any chance of hot water for an all-over body wash?"

"I need to ask Perry what our water supply is but I doubt we have enough," Krista answered as she struggled to get out of the hammock without falling. She too would love to wash her body and change her clothes.

"Here, let me give you a hand." Elaine had experience with hammocks and helped her two companions to get out and onto the floor.

"How are we for supplies, Krista – do you know?" Eugenie rolled up her sleeping bag and put it back into the bags on her motorcycle.

"From what I can see we have dry goods," Krista had been amazed that Perry had even thought of supplying them with a meal. In their travels together it had been her responsibility to see them fed. "Tea, sugar, canned milk but not much more. We ate all of the bread last night."

"That stew last night was wonderful but, if we are heading directly to Dover in this thing, I'd like a decent breakfast before we start out and perhaps something for a snack along the way." Elaine too rolled up her sleeping bag and stored it. She took all of the hammocks down and, with Eugenie on one end, began to roll them for storage.

Eugenie watched Elaine and Krista work, wanting to learn all she could about this travelling house. "After a cup of tea, we can pool our money and open a kitty. I will do a supply run."

The women all yelled when Perry opened the door in the side of the truck. The cold wind that entered through the open door was enough to shock them fully awake. They shivered where they stood.

"Get the fire on the go, ladies," Perry began to throw driftwood and seaweed into the body of the truck.

The three women rushed to remove the driftwood from the floor, grimacing at the sand that fell.

"We need to make a supply run before we take off, Perry," Krista said when all four were once more sitting at the wooden table they had set up, cups of tea in hand.

"I am hungry." Perry had made a point of having something on hand to eat for their first night camping. He had thought of tea-making supplies but he hadn't stocked the kitchen. That was work best left to the women.

"I can take my motorcycle to the local shops." Eugenie grimaced at the taste of the tea. Condensed milk was perfectly fine for emergencies but she preferred fresh milk.

"We can stock up with breakfast items and something for snacks along the way," said Elaine. "We won't need to search for places to eat and wash our hands with the amenities this truck has to offer." She had asked about the water supply – sadly there was not enough water to allow them to wash.

Chapter 7

"*What did our esteemed Mrs Fagin have to say?*" Krista called over her shoulder.

She was driving the truck with Perry in the passenger seat. Elaine and Eugenie were sitting on the floor in the back, holding onto the seat backs when necessary. They had tried sitting on the bench but slid all over, almost falling to the floor on more than one occasion whenever Krista tapped on the brakes. There had been much grumbling about 'men' when not one cushion could be found to sit on. They had made bundles of their dirty laundry wrapped around with their oil coats and used them to soften the cold floor.

"*We didn't speak for long!*" Elaine shouted over the

sound of the engine. *"The telephone was eating my money almost faster than I could get the coins into the slot."*

Elaine had been volunteered to telephone Mrs Fagin from a public telephone box. The woman needed notice of their arrival as she liked to open up and stock the cottage. A service they greatly appreciated.

"In between berating me for our absence, she did manage to tell me that the gas water-heater has been installed!" Elaine almost whooped.

"Oh, heavenly bliss!" Eugenie clapped her hands. *"A long hot bath!"*

"We will need to draw straws to see who goes first!" Krista too was delighted. No more heating pots of water on the stove and carrying them up the stairs to the bathroom.

"I hate to break into all of this joy," Perry turned to say over the back of his seat, "but our orders are to report to the castle as soon as we arrive in Dover."

"Perry," Krista never took her eyes off the road, "if you think we three are going to appear in front of a group of pretty-boy sailors, dirty, hungry, travel-stained and exhausted, you are delusional."

"What are you talking about?" Perry threw his hands in the air. "What pretty-boy sailors? You will be meeting with the top brass of the navy and the army. I thought I had told you that already. They want to speak with you."

"How do they know what time we will arrive in Dover?" Krista took one hand off the wheel to slap at Perry's chest. It was a snap action and her hand was soon back on the steering wheel. "They will have to be alerted as to the time, will they not? While we sit around the castle waiting on their pleasure. Then to add insult to injury they will all arrive polished to within an inch of their life and wearing their best uniform."

"But our orders!" Perry objected.

"You can park this thing in front of our cottage." Eugenie had come up on her knees and, holding on to the back of Perry's seat, she pushed her face into the front of the truck.

"You can telephone Rear Admiral Andrews from our cottage." Elaine too was now holding on to the back of the driver's seat. "After we three have had something to eat and drink, a long bath and washed our hair. That is not too much to ask, surely?"

"But our orders ..." Perry once again tried to object.

"Perry, you don't really believe that these men have been sitting around Dover Castle waiting for our arrival, do you?" Krista snapped. "It makes more sense to set up an actual time and place for the interview. We can't sit around the castle for hours on end, you know. We are busy women."

Elaine and Eugenie fell back onto their makeshift cushions, laughing. Krista had everything well in hand.

"Well, here we are."

Perry was in the driver's seat when they turned onto the road that ran in front of the group of cottages sitting in green fields. It was late afternoon. They had been on the road for eight hours. They had stopped in a layby to make a pot of tea and something to eat. Perry had cans of petrol to hand for emergencies but they had found several garages on their route. They had walked about to stretch their legs and changed drivers at each stop.

"I am so glad we didn't have to do that journey on our motorcycles." Eugenie groaned and stood when the truck came to a stop in front of their cottage.

"It might have been more comfortable than rolling around on the floor in the back of this thing," Elaine said.

"The two of you slept half the journey away." Krista opened the passenger door. "Don't think I didn't see you." She had been glad of the chance to question Perry about Philippe Dumas. He wouldn't say much, just enough for her to know that Philippe was now providing information and assistance to Captain Waters and his group.

"We had to do something to pass the time," Elaine said.

"Ladies," Perry was exhausted and his bad leg was aching, "I have to return this vehicle."

"Nonsense!" Krista turned around to stare at Perry. She knew he was hurting. "It will be perfectly safe here. Lock it up and come inside. I daresay you are just as tired and hungry as we are."

"You had better obey." Eugenie was standing in the back of the truck, organising her belongings. "I have noticed Krista gets very cranky if she doesn't have her nap."

They all laughed at this and without further comment began to organise their goods before leaving the truck.

The women pushed their motorcycles into the garden while Perry checked that everything was as it should be in the body of the truck.

***

"You can report in now, Perry," Krista fresh from her bath, wearing her comfortable gent's pyjamas and long woollen dressing gown, a towel around her head, stood in the open doorway of the small sitting room at the front of the cottage.

"I have your permission, do I?" Perry, his stockinged feet resting on the hearth surround in front of a blazing fire he had started, asked.

"There is no need for sarcasm, Perry." Krista walked into the room to stand warming her hands in front of the fire. "In an emergency, no doubt, we can jump to but today, well, we three really needed to return to our base and simply relax. We haven't been able to truly relax in quite a while."

"I've already reported in," Perry moved his feet out of the way. "The meeting is set for eleven in the morning which means we can all have a lie-in."

"Are you spending the night here?" Krista asked. "You are welcome to sleep on the sofa. We can pull it from under the window and put it in front of the fire. We do that sometimes in the evening. It's very comfortable."

"I was thinking of sleeping in the truck."

"There is no need for that." Krista smiled. "You might as well be warm and comfortable in here." She didn't mention that the warmth from the fire would help relax his injured leg. Perry was very sensitive about what he saw as his weakness. "You can have a bath when

Eugenie gets out. Elaine is taking care of feeding us." She laughed. "Well, Mrs Fagin is feeding us – Elaine is simply heating up the stew she left for us. There will be plenty. The woman always makes enough for an army."

"That woman's blood should be bottled." Elaine, in pyjamas and robe, her skin practically glowing from the scrubbing she gave herself, damp hair hanging straight came into the sitting room.

"I'm telling Perry he should stay the night on the couch," Krista said.

"Oh, do stay, Perry," said Elaine. "You are more than welcome."

"What will the neighbours think?" Perry had no desire to get the women into trouble with loose talk about their morals. He was a single man after all and these three were very attractive young women.

"If anyone has any objections we'll set Mrs Fagin on them." Elaine laughed. "They shouldn't be so bad-minded."

"I have my uniform in the truck." Perry was tempted.

"Bring it in and hang it in the warmth," Elaine suggested. "You don't want to be putting cold damp clothing on first thing in the morning."

"Will Eugenie agree with me staying over?" Perry asked.

"I'll ask her," Krista hurried out of the room and up the stairs. She knocked on the bathroom door and shouted her question to Eugenie who was wallowing in the bath. She had no objections.

***

"I don't know if this stew is the best thing I have ever tasted or I'm simply hungry." Perry spooned stew into his mouth, trying not to groan at the taste.

"Mrs Fagin makes a lot of fish stews for us." Krista said. "She makes the day's catch stretch to include us when she needs to – I don't know what we would do without her. I don't think any of us can cook?" She looked across at the other two females who shook their heads in denial of any knowledge of cooking. Growing up she had not been allowed in the restaurant kitchen of the Auberge – chefs, according to Madame Dumas – were men. "She also gets in supplies for us. We don't seem to have much free time to go shopping for our own needs."

"Perry," Elaine put her spoon down to look across the table at the man seated at Krista's side, "what can we expect from this meeting that has been called for the morning – do you know?"

Perry quickly swallowed his food to say, "I would only be guessing."

Eugenie stopped eating long enough to say, "Anything you can share with us would be appreciated."

"I think ... and it is only my opinion ..." Perry knew he wasn't sharing any State secrets and these women deserved to know what might be in front of them.

"Do tell us," Krista prompted.

"I don't know if you three are aware that Rear Admiral Andrews has finally – thanks in great part to you three – been granted funding for setting up units of Wrens to map possible sites for telegraph poles and radio towers."

"That is good news," Eugenie said, "but what has

that to do with tomorrow's meeting?"

"The Army and Navy have worked together to prepare that truck parked outside. There is a great deal of interest in how it can be used to move certain types of troops around the country. The Powers That Be want to pick your brains as to its usefulness." Perry looked at the women for a moment. "If it were me going before a mixed service committee, I would have a written report ready to put before them – in triplicate." He turned his head to look at Krista.

Krista groaned as all eyes turned to her. "I should never have learned to type."

"You will have time this evening to pick each other's brains as to what should go in the report." Perry pushed his empty bowl away from him. "I will be on hand to offer any advice I can." He searched through his dressing-gown pocket for his cigarettes while staring intently at the three women. "You three have blazed a trail. You have been mentioned in despatches. That means a great deal to the men at the top – believe me. You need to make note of the work you have carried out and, without sounding as if you are complaining, make note of the problems you have encountered."

"Lord," Elaine stood to begin clearing the table, "where to start?"

Eugenie too stood. "I'll wash the dishes and leave them to drain while we enjoy a cup of tea and a cigarette."

"I'll make tea and coffee," Elaine offered.

"I suppose I had better fetch my shorthand notebook and a load of pencils." Krista almost sighed.

"Now that is what I like." Perry put a match to his cigarette. He looked at the women with a wide smile on his face. "Women jumping to, while the poor male takes his ease with his cigarette."

Elaine threw a dishtowel at his head.

Eugenie, with a dramatic gasp of outrage, took the cigarette from his hands and put it to her own lips.

Krista laughed and left the room to seek the items she needed.

Chapter 8

"Well, look what the wind blew in!" Mary Black smiled when she saw the three women standing in the large office in Dover Castle set aside for the use of the Wrens. "We thought you three had disappeared off the face of the earth. Give me a minute to put my jacket and hat on. We can go to the NAAFI for a cup of tea and a gossip. You will have to suffer, I'm afraid, Krista – there are no coffee drinkers here."

The three women were wearing their dress uniform skirts so as not to shock the males. Eugenie had polished their navy lace-up shoes until they gleamed. She had brushed their uniforms until not a particle of dust would have dared to land on them. The woman was a marvel with a bristle brush. They were each wearing sheer stockings, however – they had no need of thick-knit stockings at this point. Perry had whistled in admiration when he'd seen them. Then he'd driven them to the castle and left them. He had to return the truck and report in.

"Mary," Krista said, "I need to borrow a typewriter." She looked around the open space of the office and didn't see any typewriters on display.

"We have a typing pool now, I'm proud to say." Mary laughed. "Our esteemed leader Wren Superintendent Andrews has been very demanding. She is a marvel to observe. That woman has the bit well and truly between her teeth. She has demanded all kinds of things for the Wrens – and she has been given them."

"If you'll point me towards the typing pool?" Krista had to get her notes typed up – in triplicate – before they attended the meeting called for this morning. If she was very lucky they would have a stencilling machine available which would save her a lot of bother.

"While Krista does her work I'd love tea and a catch-up, Mary," said Elaine.

"I feel guilty dumping the work on you, Krista, but I can't type unfortunately," said Eugenie. "I too would love to hear all of the latest, Mary."

The four women, dressed in their Wren uniforms, marched down the hallway of the castle. It wasn't far from the office to a large well-lit room that, when Mary opened the door, rang with the sound of typewriter keys being hit. The sound of bells as the carriages of the typewriters reached the end and had to be returned was practically music.

Mary led them to a woman at the front of the room.

"Ladies, this is Esther Prescott – she is responsible for keeping order in the typing pool. Esther, I just need a minute to speak to the Wrens, if you will allow me."

She turned away from the woman's desk without waiting for permission. She outranked Esther.

"*Wrens!*" Mary clapped her hands – all movement stopped.

The women were seated at desks that stretched across the spacious room with walkways from one end of the room to the other, allowing space to either leave your desk or for someone to march along examining the work being carried out.

"Allow me to introduce you all to Leading Wrens Strange, Green and Wood. If at any time these ladies request your assistance, feel free to put all other work aside and tend to their wants." She searched the room, looking for a particular typist. It was difficult with the hours the Wrens were keeping to know who was on site at any given time. Ah, there she was!

"Nixon, you can help Strange," Mary said when she found the Wren she was looking for. "Nixon is our best typist, Krista. You don't have to do the work yourself. Nixon could have it ready for you in no time."

Krista smiled. "Thank you, but I think I'd prefer to borrow Wren Nixon's typewriting machine – if she could be allowed to stay by my side and assist me. I don't know where the paper and stencil equipment are kept." She wanted everyone to leave so she could chat in private with Vicky Nixon. She had trained in shorthand and typing with the red-haired green-eyed Vicky in London. She was beyond delighted to see her here. They had so much to talk about. The noise of the typewriters when they started up again should allow them to keep their conversation private.

"Very well," Mary said. "Wren Nixon, supply any and all assistance to leading Wren Strange." She turned then and smiled at Elaine and Eugenie. "If you two will follow me, I'll show you to the NAAFI."

The three women left the room while Krista hurried along the space between the desks to reach Vicky's desk at the back of the room.

Krista stood by Vicky's desk, looking at the women still sitting with their hands folded. "As you were, Wrens, do not allow me to interrupt your work." She turned her back to the room to smile so widely at Vicky that her face hurt.

"How may I help you, Leading Wren?" Vicky's green eyes were sparkling.

"Do we have a stencil copying machine available for our use?" Krista crossed her fingers. With the amount of admiralty office work being carried out at Dover Castle there must be at least one copying machine somewhere in the building. Any and all copying machines would be too large and noisy for this room. She really hoped they had one – it would save so much work.

"We do, Leading Wren Strange, but it is housed in a designated room along the hallway," Vicky said. "I could show you."

"If you would be so kind." Krista stepped to one side to allow Vicky to leave her desk.

"Follow me." Vicky took a moment to notify the Wren in charge of the room and they left.

"Vicky!" Krista didn't even wait for her friend to close the door firmly at their backs before grabbing her. The two women danced on the spot. They had to keep their cries of joy stifled in case anyone stuck their head in the door to see what on earth was going on. "It is so good to see you. And a Wren – I am so happy for you!"

"Do you really need a copying machine?" Vicky didn't want to get into trouble. It was wonderful to see Krista again but the Wrens in the typing pool were kept under strict supervision.

"I do." Krista noticed that her friend's speech was much improved since the last time they spoke. She didn't mention it now. She was so thankful to have a stencil machine available to her. She intended to type her report onto a special thickly waxed paper. The typewriter keys would cut an impression into the wax. The pages would be attached to the inked wheel of the copying machine and as many copies as were needed could be printed off. In her opinion far superior to carbon paper. The copies would come off the machine pristine and easily read.

"Do you want me to show you how to work the machine?" There were a selection of stencil copying machines on the market, each with different working parts.

"No, thanks." Krista laughed. "But you can check

each page I type when it comes off the machine, if you would." She looked around the room for a moment. "It will give us an excuse to spend time together. Now, quickly, tell me everything. It is so long since I received a letter from you. I was beginning to worry I had insulted you unforgivably."

"By telling Miss Andrews all about me?" Vicky laughed.

"I wanted to help. You had your heart set on joining the Wrens." Krista had listened to Vicky's dreams when they were doing the course together.

"My heart was broken when our headmistress Miss Huxley told me I would never be accepted into the Wrens because I was of the wrong social class and had a strong London accent. I was angry too. It wasn't fair."

"So, Miss Andrews was able to help you?" Krista had made a point of telling Miss Andrews all about Vicky Nixon. Vicky had been the top of their class in everything. She was exactly what Miss Andrews wanted for her Wrens. There was but one problem – Vicky's strong London accent.

"God help me, the woman is a dictator!" Vicky's laughing green eyes belied her words. "She telephoned the house demanding I present myself before her with the final results of my examinations in hand. Then she met with my mother and sat in our kitchen barking out orders. She had me mam and me shivering in our shoes." Vicky's speech lapsed for a moment at the final sentence.

"You sound now like you have a plum in your mouth." Krista smiled. "She obviously helped you."

"Helped!" Vicky almost yelped. "She was wonderful.

She gave me some of the British Broadcasting Corporation (BBC) tapes she taught you English with and everyone always did say that you sounded like someone off the wireless. The lady lodgers my mother houses helped me with my diction. When you wrote of learning to march about the place, I had my dad teach me and my brothers to march and salute. It was hard work but with me mam and dad's help we turned it into a game."

"I am so glad you managed to achieve your dream." Krista wanted to clap her hands in joy. "I bet your father is proud of you."

"The family supported me a great deal." Vicky's smile was sad.

Krista couldn't question her friend here and now but she wondered what had cast that shadow over her face. Surely not the mention of her father? Vicky always spoke with such high praise of the man she called "me da".

"I got a job with a local shipbuilder and with my mother's blessings was able to use my wages to buy decent outfits at the market just like you suggested. By the time I was called for my interview with the Wrens, I was ready. I had everything down pat. It helped a great deal to know Miss Andrews and she suggested I use her name as a reference. I was shaking in my shoes, I can tell you. I worried I'd slip up when I spoke but if I talk real slow I can manage. I do lose the plum when I get excited." She shrugged. "When they tested my typing and shorthand – I was in."

"I am so happy for you, Vicky."

"What about you?" Vicky asked. "I thought you

couldn't join the Wrens – being French and all?" She'd been surprised to see her friend wearing a Leading Wren's uniform. She knew from her letters that Krista was working and training with the Wrens but she hadn't known she was a bloomin' Leading Wren.

"Special Service Wren." Krista pointed to the braid on the cuff of her jacket. "We better get these documents typed up. I have a meeting with the brass at eleven and need to give them my report."

"Come on," Vicky opened the door of the room and stepped out. "We can set up a time to get together. I am at the Wrennery with the rest of the Wrens."

"I'll give you the telephone number of the cottage I'm staying in – I don't know when I'll be there but we have to get together and talk. I am so glad to see you, Vicky."

The two women walked down the hall and back into the typing pool. Vicky went to a tall supply cupboard and began to assemble what Krista would need to cut a stencil.

Krista took a sheet of waxed paper carefully from Vicky's hand, aware she had to be careful not to crack the wax. She took a seat in front of Vicky's typewriter, rolled the paper into the machine, laid her notes close to hand on the desktop, and with fingers flying began to type. She was aware of the curiosity of the women in the room but she was cutting it fine if she wanted a report to hand out at the upcoming meeting.

"Will you be needing each report placed in a folder, Leading Wren Lestrange?" Vicky was the picture of efficiency as she stood waiting for the first page to leave the machine.

"That would be ideal." Krista's fingers never stopped moving. "Thank you."

"How many copies will you need?" Vicky asked.

Krista thought for a moment. Perry had said that all of the services would be represented at the upcoming meeting. The forms should be in triplicate he'd said, so, three each for the navy, army and air force. "I need three copies for each arm of the services, and an additional one for me personally. So, ten copies in all. If there is a way to protect the wax copy – stop it from cracking – I would appreciate having the wax copy also."

The two women worked together smoothly. As Krista finished typing one waxed page, Vicky took it and checked it for typing errors – finding none, she carried the page down the hall to the copying machine. She returned with ten printed copies of the page. There was a long table set in front of the typing-pool windows which was used for collating documents. Vicky spread the pages out before taking the next page. In this way Krista soon had ten folders – one with her name written on the file folder – with beautifully typed reports inside, to carry with her into the meeting with the men in charge.

Vicky was enjoying herself. It made a nice break from sitting in front of the typewriter all day.

The last page Krista typed, on standard paper, had her address and the telephone number of the cottage. She passed this to Vicky with no one being the wiser. She wasn't sure what the rules were for fraternisation between Wren ranks but thought it best to err on the side of caution.

"Thank you so much, Wren Nixon." Krista gathered the folders up in her arms. "You have been an enormous help. It is much appreciated."

"You are welcome." Vicky took her seat before her typewriter demurely.

Krista stopped at the front desk to thank the typing-pool supervisor, making sure to comment on what a very efficient and helpful Wren Vicky Nixon was. She gave a nod of her head to the women typing away on their machines and hurried from the typing pool. She hoped the other three Wrens were still in the NAAFI. She could use a hot drink even if it was tea.

Chapter 9

Krista stepped into the NAAFI with the folders under her arm. She grabbed a cup of tea from the serving counter. There appeared to be a great many men in the NAAFI for the time of day. The khaki of army uniforms mixed with the dark-blue naval uniforms. Wasn't that rather unusual? She ignored the shouts and whistles at her appearance and joined her friends at their table.

"What have I missed?" She pulled out a chair and put the folders on the seat before pulling out another chair to sit on.

"We haven't had a great deal of time for gossip, I'm afraid," Mary Black leaned in to say. "We have been taking note of the uniforms and insignia the men in this room are wearing. There are army, air force and naval men in this room – most unusual."

"Anyone know what is going on?" Krista asked.

"I nabbed one of our Wrens before we came in here!" Mary whispered. "I don't know if you are aware but our Wrens are being allowed to serve in the officers' mess. Wren Walters is on duty today. She told me that she had never seen so much gold braid in her life. What on earth is going on? Does it have anything to do with you three? I have asked this pair," she nodded towards Elaine and Eugenie, "but they can tell me nothing. What is in that report you are carrying?"

The women leaned in to better hear each other, ignoring the unsavoury comments being shouted at them from the men grouped around the room. Not all of the men, it had to be said, but enough to ruin any idea of relaxing.

"I know nothing." Krista sipped her tea. "We three were ordered to present ourselves here this morning. We have no idea why or indeed what it is about. If there is something going on, I doubt it has anything to do with us."

"I need to be aware of what is going on in and around the castle," Mary Black said. "It is vital I protect and promote the Wrens in my charge. It is not easy as we are resented and kept out of the workings of the castle. We are allowed to type, clean and serve at table." She sighed deeply. "That is not what I signed up for."

The piercing sound of a bosun's whistle cut off all sound.

"*Leading Wren Greenwood – attention!*" a male voice barked.

Elaine jumped to her feet and stood proudly at attention, her heart almost beating out of her chest but her face serene.

"*Follow me!*" Without waiting, the sailor turned and quick-marched out of the NAAFI.

The three Wrens watched their friend march out with her head in the air. As soon as the door closed at her back a wave of sound moved over the NAAFI as whispers and speculations were exchanged around the room.

"I don't know how I am supposed to run this unit if I don't know what is going on!" Mary practically wailed. "I am kept in the dark, then when they need a Wren I am supposed to know what is going on and supply the best candidate for the job. How on earth can I work efficiently from a position of ignorance?"

"Mary," Eugenie felt sorry for the woman, "I don't know where Green has gone and am concerned. As far as running the Wren unit here at the castle," she spread her arms wide, "I am completely the wrong person to consult."

"We are out and about all of the time, Mary." Krista's eyes were on the door Elaine had gone through, worried for her friend. "The only contact we have had has been with the very disagreeable Commander Tate and Rear Admiral Andrews."

"I have had dealings with Tate and been tempted to see if his head is really as hard as it looks." Mary had to restrain herself from punching Tate on more than one occasion.

"We need to go to our meeting." Krista gulped at the time on the large clock on the NAAFI wall. "And we have no idea where the meeting is taking place." She looked at Eugenie. "What should we do about Green? She is to be at the meeting too."

"That is typical of how we are being treated here." Mary wanted to kick something. "We are not given the information we need, then when we fail to turn up or are late we receive male smirks and condescension. It is enough to make one spit."

The door to the NAAFI opened and all eyes turned to the opening. Perry stood in the doorway, picture-book perfect in his special forces khaki army uniform, the braid of his office gleaming on his jacket and cap.

Krista felt her heart skip a beat. Perry presented an image of masculine perfection that could be used on recruitment posters.

"*Strange, Wood, front and centre on the double!*" Perry didn't step into the room.

He was an officer – a lieutenant to judge by his insignia – and wouldn't be welcome in the serving man's NAAFI.

"We will talk more later, Mary." Eugenie stepped smartly away from the table.

"If I might suggest," Krista whispered to Mary as she leaned over to take the folders from the chair seat, "make an appointment to consult with Rear Admiral Andrews. He may have some advice to offer you on the best way to handle the Powers That Be." Not waiting for a response, she followed Eugenie in marching smartly from the NAAFI.

Mary Black watched silently. Things were going to

have to change around here. She was in charge of the Wrens and needed to be made aware of anything that affected them.

"Perry, a lieutenant?" Krista remarked as the three quick-marched in step down the long white-painted tunnels, moving ever deeper under Dover Castle. She worried about Eugenie – the poor woman's face was pasty white and her breathing erratic.

Eugenie tried to control her breathing. Her childhood doctor had diagnosed claustrophobia and suggested she might grow out of it. Well, that hadn't come to pass. She hadn't grown very tall and she still suffered horribly.

"Rank has its privileges. It helps too when dealing with the men," Perry replied. "You have noticed that yourself, Leading Wren Strange, I have no doubt."

"We need to find Green." Krista ignored his remark. They could not discuss such things here and now.

"Captain Greenwood requested a private meeting with his daughter." Perry's feet never lost their beat.

"Elaine's father is here?" Krista's feet lost their rhythm.

Perry took her elbow, his fingers pressing into her flesh, and almost jerked her back into step.

"*Sir!*" A young midshipman saluted Perry smartly, ignoring the women. "If you would follow me."

The sailor stepped around Perry, Krista and Eugenie heading back in the direction – Krista fervently hoped – of the tunnel exit.

"Where are we going?" Perry fell into step with the midshipman.

"Sir, the meeting has been moved to a different vessel."

Krista ignored the two men, concentrating on Eugenie who was pasty-faced and sweating. "Can you hold your nerve, Wood?" She stepped close to Eugenie.

"By the skin of my teeth." Eugenie hated what she perceived as her own weakness.

"Would it help if you closed your eyes?" Krista knew Eugenie didn't fear darkness.

"I would fall flat on my face."

"No, you wouldn't, not if we march in step." Krista checked the direction of the two men. There were many rooms set into the tunnels but the midshipman seemed to be heading towards the tunnel exit. She crossed her fingers, hoping she was correct in her assumption. "Drop your hand – grab my fingers."

"We can't hold hands!" Eugenie was gasping, fighting for each breath.

Krista grabbed Eugenie's little finger and pinched the flesh hard enough to cause pain. "Close your eyes. I'll guide you. Now in time – *left – left – I had a good job and I left – left…*"

In this fashion Krista led her quivering friend along the tunnel. At last she saw daylight pouring in through an exterior door which, for the moment, was standing open with sailors, air force and army privates entering and exiting. It hurt her to see her friend – so fearless in the open air – reduced to a quivering wreck.

"Open your eyes, we're almost there."

"I can take it from here, sailor." Perry stopped

walking as soon as all four people had stepped out of the tunnel and into the fresh air. He had been aware of the drama taking place behind him. He knew of Wood's claustrophobia. He had left Wood to Krista, keeping the bright-eyed midshipman's attention on himself.

"My orders are to escort you aboard the vessel, sir." The midshipman stood to attention before Perry.

Krista, thankful for even a moment in the fresh air for Eugenie, tried not to roll her eyes to heaven. She found the navy's insistence on referring to everything and anything in ship-speak slightly ludicrous. She released her tight grip on Eugenie's finger and stepped away, watching in admiration as Eugenie took deep grateful breaths of the salt-laden fresh air.

The four marched out smartly across the land leading from the tunnels to the castle. Eugenie sucking great gulps of air in through her nose and out through her mouth.

"*Lieutenant Fotheringham Carter!*" Krista called loudly in her best BBC announcer's voice. Well, enough people had told her she sounded like someone off the wireless – might as well use any advantage she might have.

"Leading Wren Strange?" Perry stopped.

"Would it be possible for us Wrens to visit the powder room?" Krista knew she was being outrageous but Eugenie needed time to recover from her shock. "One does so like to look one's best when facing superior officers." Why not use the men's prejudice against them? If they wanted to think of women as fluff-heads – well, then, she would act the part.

"*Women!*" Perry spit out in feigned disgust. He knew what she was doing and wanted to kiss her for her fast thinking. Wood looked dreadful. She couldn't go before a mixed services board looking as she did now. "We will take the long way around the castle, sailor. I believe there is a special room set aside for situations such as this." With a heavy sigh he turned and began to stroll along a path that would circle the body of the castle and allow them to remain outdoors.

"But, sir ..." The midshipman had his orders.

"I will sort it with the brass, sailor." Perry continued to stroll along.

"Krista – I am so sorry," Eugenie leaned over the porcelain sink, her white-knuckled fingers clutching the sink lip, desperately trying to breathe away her panic. She looked down at the top of Krista's head. Her friend was bent at the waist, rooting through the cupboards underneath the sinks.

The two women had stepped gratefully into the large white-with-gold-accents-tiled rooms set aside for the use of females visiting the castle. It was never intended for service women. Out of the corner of her eye Krista saw a room with a pink velvet fainting couch sitting proudly surrounded by floor-length mirrors. She wished she could have Eugenie stretch out for a moment but there was no time.

"I thought so!" She stood, proudly brandishing two soft pink face towels. "All the comforts of a hotel." She turned the hot-water tap on and held one of the towels underneath the flow. She pressed it into Eugenie's hands. "Wipe your face quickly," she ordered while putting the second towel under the cold running water. She removed the excess moisture from the towel and, lifting her friend's fine blonde hair, draped the towel over her neck.

"What am I going to do, Krista?" Eugenie's words were muffled by the damp cloth she was using to scrub at her face. "I cannot go into those tunnels – the white walls with all of that black electrical tape stretching endlessly – it makes me sick – the walls move."

"We can discuss that later." Krista had to snap Eugenie out of her funk. They had a meeting to attend. "For the moment concentrate on improving your appearance. We will be late!"

Chapter 10

"Perhaps we should have requested a stick of chalk to mark our passage," Krista muttered to Eugenie. Linking fingers again, they were following Perry and the seaman sent to guide them through a veritable warren of corridors and hallways. "How on earth are we supposed to find our way out of here?"

"I was thinking breadcrumbs, like Hansel and Gretel!" Eugenie was forcing her feet to move. Did every blessed thing they did have to be in dark dank places? She had joined the Wrens to serve her country with visions of the open seas in mind. Not this personal nightmare.

"I am trying to get a sense of where we are." Krista slowed her steps. If she wasn't much mistaken that was an arrow slot coming up. The castle, after all, was a medieval fortress. It would have been defended at one time with bow and arrow. She stepped over to the opening and looked down. "We are walking around the buildings inside the curtain wall that protects the castle."

"If we don't get out of here soon I may be tempted to jump out one of these windows!" Eugenie snapped.

"You would be the only person I know able to fit out those narrow openings." Krista laughed.

"This way is faster than trying to move among the seamen and equipment being moved into the castle." The sailor leading them opened a door to the outside and revealed a scene of organised chaos.

The castle bailey was covered with men carrying equipment while others shouted orders and instructions.

"We are going to be late to the scheduled meeting," Krista said as they were led towards a two-storey freestanding granite building, with thankfully many windows.

The chaos continued inside the building. All four people stepped smartly out of the way of men carrying rolls of cable.

"*Watson, where have you been?*" a sweating seaman in a navy boiler suit shouted at their escort. "I didn't think it would take you this long to find one army lieutenant and bring him here. Hurry up! I need you here."

"Yes, sarge." Their escort didn't try to defend the delay. He turned to the three people with him and, with a "This way, please," led them towards one of the doors off the frantic scene. He knocked loudly and waited.

"Enter!"

The door opened to a well-lit room, revealing their missing friend Elaine and, by his resemblance and captain's uniform, a man who must be her father. Rear Admiral Andrews – Reggie to his Wrens – was also present. A fire burned brightly in the room which was in a state of disorder. It was neither one thing nor the other. There was furniture that would have graced a plush lounge pushed to one side. In the centre of the room boxes and chests stood unopened. A stack of folding chairs leaned against one wall. The two older men in full naval uniform were standing by the furthest wall smoking cigars, leaving a haze of smoke hanging in the air. Elaine was standing by a window that she must have cracked open to allow the smoke to escape.

"Thank you, seaman, that will be all!" Reggie barked.

"*Sir!*" Their escort executed a neat about-face and left them.

"Enter and shut the door," Reggie said.

"Sir," Krista stepped forward to say, "we are already late for a meeting that was called for this morning."

Eugenie hurried to stand with Elaine by the window.

Perry shut the door and waited to see what was about to happen.

"Strange, welcome to the services." Reggie sighed deeply. It took time to become accustomed to the 'hurry up and wait' mentality of service life. "That meeting has been postponed for the foreseeable future. You have seen the state of the castle, have you not?" He didn't wait for a response, waving a hand towards the boxes and crates in the centre of the room. "This place is a danger to life and limb."

"Yes, sir," Krista said.

"Allow me to introduce my father to you," Elaine said, not sure of the protocol called for here. She and Krista were not fully Wrens and Perry was from a naval family but wearing army uniform. Still, surely the basic social good manners should apply. "My father Captain Henry Greenwood. Dad, these are my friends and co-workers, Krista Lestrange, Eugenie Carpenter, also known as Strange and Wood, and I don't know if you are familiar with Peregrine Fotheringham Carter?"

"Any relation –" Captain Greenwood began.

"His son," Perry supplied the information before a discussion could be entered into.

"In an army uniform?" Greenwood stared.

"Yes, sir." Perry briefly wondered if there was a sign he could sew onto his uniform to curtail the seemingly constant need to defend his position and heritage.

"Strange," Reggie cut across the chatter, "what have you got there?" He gestured towards the files Krista had clutched to her chest.

"We were asked to supply a detailed report of our work and give our impression of the vehicle the lieutenant drove to pick us up, sir. I typed the report and copied it, sir."

"Pass them to Fotheringham Carter!" Reggie snapped. "Those things make you look like a damn secretary – which you are not!" It was important to underline the service these women provided. He did not want anyone judging them as less than they were – his private force. His units would be formed of the best of the best and these three were just the beginning.

"What would you like me to do with them, sir?" Perry took the files from Krista.

"Carry them!" Reggie snapped.

A rap on the door sounded loud in the room.

"*Enter!*" Reggie shouted.

"Sub Lieutenant Riordan, rear admiral." The door was pushed open. "Your cabins are ready, sir."

"Lead the way, Riordan!" Reggie snapped, biting back the words 'It's about bloody time.' "Everyone, with me." He stepped forward smartly, eager to examine his domain.

The group were escorted across the wide hallway, being careful to avoid stepping on or tripping over the wires and machinery scattered around. Sailors stepped out of their way.

"This room is for your staff." The sub-lieutenant swept a hand around a large bright room set out with empty desks, chairs and rows of battleship-grey filing cabinets lining the walls. "Engineering will need a list of your equipment requirements at your convenience, rear admiral." He walked through the room towards an open door. "This one is a secretary's or assistant's office."

The room had no window. Two desks faced each other, leaving a walkway towards another door. Perry dropped the files he held onto one of the desks.

"Your office, rear admiral." The room was large and bright with only a large desk in it at the moment. There was a fireplace with a fire burning what appeared to be blocks of wood.

"Thank you, sub-lieutenant." Reggie gave a jerk of his head towards the open door. "That will be all." He waited until the sub-lieutenant had closed the door at his back before looking at the people who had accompanied him. "What am I supposed to do with all of this? I can run a battleship with well-trained men under my command – but how on earth am I supposed to know what I need to run this ship? That is what a second officer and a supplies officer are for." He opened his arms wide, looking around the room with a bewildered expression not often seen on his face.

"Where is Commander Tate?" Kristen looked around the bare room. Surely the rear admiral's books and such should already be in place. Where were the maps, telephones and radios he would need?

"Because of his knowledge of the German language and parts of Germany, Tate has been moved from my command," Reggie was pleased to announce. "There is no point in all of us sticking around here like barnacles on a hull."

"I have a staff car here, Reggie." Captain Greenwood had never seen his commander and friend act like this – he didn't envy the man the situation he found himself in. Still, it was his understanding that Reggie had brought this on himself. He had fought to be given the control of Wren special forces. On his own head be it now. "Why don't I take the Wrens back to their ship?"

"Good man." Reggie looked around. "You can take

your daughter and Wood. Strange and Army will remain here." He glared at Perry. "Where are the files you were holding for me?"

"I put them on one of the desks in the secretary's office, sir."

"Get them."

Perry held the door open for Captain Greenwood, Elaine and Eugenie to leave.

Krista watched him step into the outer office to retrieve the files she'd so carefully typed and copied.

"Pull two chairs over to the desk, Strange." Reggie wanted to kick something. He had given no thought to the actual nuts and bolts of this strange new ship he was expected to sail. He had his office in the tunnels for his use when he was in Dover. What was he supposed to do with all of this space?

Perry stepped into the room with the files.

"Shut the door," Reggie ordered. "You can put the files on the desk." He walked around the desk, pulled the leather office chair away from it and sat. He leaned forward, pushed the files out of his way, and stared at the two young people now sitting in front of him.

"I have heard good things about the pair of you from Captain Waters." He waited but neither said a word. "What is said in this cabin must remain in this cabin unless I give you express permission to discuss my affairs outside this ship."

"Yes, sir," Perry said.

"Sir." Krista gave a nod.

"This base," Reggie waved his arms around in a

gesture meant to encompass all of Dover castle, "will be a key location in the war. Men and machinery are being moved here as you have seen. There will be a great deal of intelligence and information-gathering going on under these many roofs. The tunnels will play a key role. As such I need to be here."

Perry and Krista waited.

"I need help rigging up my ship for maximum efficiency. The first thing I need is a way to make a pot of tea or coffee without having to resort to calling the NAAFI every time I need something hot to drink, for goodness' sake! I haven't even been issued a telephone yet as you can see." He slapped his hand on the desktop. "I haven't had time to go through a list of men available to help me set up. I don't want another like Tate – unable to bend – judging everything. I need a good man to run this ship day to day."

Perry and Krista exchanged a look but said nothing.

"You two have been asked to perform some unusual tasks – have you any advice you might offer?" He wasn't too proud to ask.

"Reggie," Krista sat forward on her seat, hoping she wasn't overstepping but the man had asked, "the person to ask for help is a member of your own family. Violet can give you every assistance and provide the staff you need."

"Women!" Reggie wanted to bury his face in his hands. Violet would crow if he had to ask for her help.

"*Wrens*," Krista snapped.

"Rear admiral," Perry began.

"Within these walls call me Reggie."

"Thank you and I am Perry."

"Very well, Perry, say what is on your mind."

"Reggie," he almost choked, thinking of his father's reaction if he knew his son was addressing a rear admiral so familiarly, "you have said you have heard of Krista and me – does that mean you have read reports?" He needed to know what this man knew.

"I know of your mission into Belgium and Germany." Reggie put his elbows on the desk. "Waters and I agree that it is past time that all branches of the services share information. We are not alone in this belief. The Powers That Be are setting up a central intelligence agency. We will need all the information we can lay our hands on."

"Yes, sir." Perry would be part of that agency when it was in place. "The news coming out of Europe is beyond distressing. In some cases unbelievable. It is only the knowledge that the person sharing the information with us is an actual eye witness that forces us to believe what we hear. Krista and I witnessed what the newspapers are calling Kristallnacht."

"Shocking!" Reggie shook his head at the horrors being inflicted on men, women and children.

"Sir, it goes beyond anything we can conceive of," Perry said. "We are not ready as a nation for what Hitler will throw at us. This war will be unlike anything ever seen before."

"Your point?" Reggie knew he must have one. He had heard good things about this Fotheringham Carter son.

"This war will take years to fight. All able-bodied men will be called on to play their part. Start as you mean to go on, Reggie. There is no point in training men to work under your command – in a fashion of your design – only to have them removed when there is a need. The women you choose to carry out your work in recent months have performed impressively." He gave a nod towards Krista. "The Wrens are an impressive bunch of women. Your own sister and my mother are two very capable women. They can help you set up using a force that will *not* be removed from your command as the needs of the war change."

"I hadn't thought of using only female sailors." Reggie had used the women as an example to inspire midshipmen to try and out-perform his females. Had he outsmarted himself?

"You will have need of men to drive the adapted trucks," Perry said. "Only until you can train the women to drive perhaps but for the moment drivers will be a necessity. So, Reggie –

A rap on the door stopped all speech.

The door opened without the person who had knocked waiting for permission to enter. Clarence Brownlow-Hastings – the man Krista knew as Mr Brown – stepped into the office.

Perry and Krista jumped to their feet.

"What on earth is happening around here? I have been forced to actually search for you amongst what I can only call mayhem. If I had not encountered Captain Greenwood on his way out of here, I would still be searching. Allow me to tell you, my good man – I am not impressed."

"I am not exactly delighted myself, Clarence." Reggie stood. He would not give Clarence Brownlow-Hastings the opportunity to look down his nose at him.

Krista stared at the man standing behind her bogeyman. It was Sylvester Stowe-Grenville, Baron Sturbridge – what was he doing here and in the company of her Grey Man?

Chapter 11

"What are you doing here?" Krista was perched on the edge of one of the many desks in the staff room.

Krista, Perry and Sylvester had been ejected from Reggie's office by the Grey Man. He had escorted them from the room through the area designated for two secretaries before slamming the door into this large room shut. The sound of shouting male voices was muffled by the space between the offices and the closed doors.

"Krista …" Perry, leaning against a desk, jerked his chin towards Sylvester.

"Sorry. Peregrine Fotheringham Carter – the admiral's son – meet Sylvester Stowe Grenville, Baron Sturbridge – the Duke of Stowe-Grenville's great-grandson." Perry was a member of the upper crust. He would recognise the Duke's name. "Now that we have your names and antecedents out of the way, I repeat – *what in heaven's name are you doing here, Sylvester, and wearing a special forces uniform?*"

A nod of his head in Perry's direction was all the reaction Sylvester gave to the introduction.

"*This is all your fault,*" he bit out through clenched teeth at Krista. "I took those blasted papers you were so concerned about to Scotland Yard and, before I could take a deep breath, I was bundled out of there and carted off in the back of a police vehicle like a common criminal!"

Perry leaned against a desk, his arms folded across his chest, and watched the pair glare at each other. It amused him to imagine that there was almost a resemblance between their clenched jaws.

"They took you to the Grey Man?" Krista asked.

"I beg your pardon?" Sylvester frowned.

"*Him!*" Krista threw one arm towards the sound of raised voices. "The man in there with the rear admiral." She had only ever known him as Mr Brown but thought of him always as the Grey Man. Her bogeyman – a man who frightened her and invaded her nightmares.

"Oh, you are speaking of old Clarence!" Sylvester nodded. "Yes, that was a stroke of good fortune. Clarence Brownlow Hastings to give him his full title. The man is a friend of the family, don't you know – engaged to marry a paternal cousin at one time – he soon took me in hand – been a great help to me."

"Perhaps ..." Perry began only to be interrupted by the opening of the door off the room and the appearance of the rear admiral and Clarence Brownlow Hastings.

"Krista, get this area organised!" the rear admiral barked as he practically marched across the long room. He slammed the folders he carried into Perry's chest. "File these somewhere safe. We will need to be able to put our hands on them – later."

Perry clutched the files, stopping them falling to the floor.

"I will be back shortly." He stopped and looked back with the door handle in his hand. "Be certain to organise tea and a bottle of something strong and alcoholic."

Perry and Sylvester had come to attention.

"You two," Brownlow Hastings said, "assist her."

The two men stepped out into the hallway and the door closed.

The three in the room remained standing, staring at each other.

"What am I supposed to do with these," Perry stared at the folders.

"I spent a lot of time getting those darn files ready." Krista took the folders. "I'm not going to shove them into any of these file cabinets. With the way things are going around here, the cabinets might be moved before we return." She carried the files into the room set aside for a secretary and put the files into one of the desk drawers. She put the file with her name on top of the stack before closing the drawer. Hopefully, if anyone discovered these files before she returned – they would be returned to her.

She slapped her hands together. "You two follow me. I haven't a clue how to set up an office. I don't even know where the NAAFI serving this area is!" She threw her hands dramatically into the air. "But I know where to get help if I can find my way around this place."

"Mary, I need help." Krista had suggested that Perry and Sylvester talk to the men in and around the castle – do a little reconnoitring. She had come to throw herself on the Wrens' mercy – Mary Black in particular.

"You look like someone in need of a drink." Mary smiled. "I'll have Wren Stevens brew up a pot of tea. That's the best I can offer, I'm afraid." She pushed a button on the intercom on her desk. She held the button down and spoke into the machine to order the tea. "Now, tell me how I can help."

Krista poured out her problem into Mary's sympathetic ears, ending with a shake of her head just as Wren Stevens rapped on the office door.

"Thank you, Stevens, we will serve ourselves." Mary Black was picking up the handset of her telephone.

"Yes, ma'am." Stevens put the tray on the top of Mary's wide desk and left the office.

Krista leaned forward to stare at the cups, saucers, milk jug, sugar bowl, slop bowl, teapot and a plate of biscuits that sat on the tray. Where on earth had these come from? There had not been time to travel into the tunnels to the only NAAFI she was aware of. Was there a NAAFI in the castle itself? She needed to know these things.

"I'm waiting to be put through to Wren Superintendent Andrews." Mary, with the handset to her ear, nodded when Krista held up the teapot. "The demand for Wrens has increased dramatically in recent months. I know of some that could help you set up an office for Rear Admiral Andrews but they are on other duties at the moment." She lodged the telephone handset between her shoulder and jaw and took the teacup and saucer from Krista's hand. "If you need women who are not afraid of hard physical work, our friend Eugenie should have an idea of three-day-eventers who have joined up. Those women won't be afraid of being out in the elements and getting dirty."

Krista sipped her tea while Mary explained her predicament to Violet Andrews over the telephone. She gulped her tea and jumped to her feet when the telephone handset was held out towards her.

"Hello," she said into the mouthpiece. She was never sure how to address the woman who had been her English teacher for years in France and now claimed a familial interest in her.

"Krista!" Violet Andrews voice barked from the telephone. "What is that brother of mine up to now? I thought he was engaged in hush-hush operations. Why does he need office staff?"

"Rear Admiral Andrews has been given large offices in the grounds of the castle. At the moment the rooms are furnished with desks, filing cabinets and chairs only.

I have been ordered to set up the premises and I have no idea how to go about the task I've been set. How do I go about ordering the equipment and personnel required? I don't even know what is needed!"

"Honestly, we are Wrens not magicians." Violet Andrews tutted.

"The Grey Man is here."

"Your Mr Brown?" Violet had heard a great deal about the man Krista referred to as the Grey Man. "Is he indeed?"

"He is in company with Sylvester Stowe Grenville," Krista heard the other woman gasp. She had told Violet about her encounter with Sylvester.

"How interesting," Violet said softly. "Let me clear a few matters from my desk here and I'll be down to speak with you. Thankfully Kent is not that far from London. Do what you can until I arrive." The telephone line went dead.

"Wren Superintendent Andrews is coming down." Krista passed the handset back to Mary. She hoped Violet wasn't coming to gloat over her high-ranking brother's need of her Wrens.

"Probably for the best." Mary Black picked up the teapot. "She has the authority we need to commandeer whatever might be needed."

Perry stepped into the office. "I'm sorry to interrupt but, Krista, we need to go."

"Thank you for your help, Mary." Krista jumped to her feet and followed after Perry. Sylvester was waiting in the hall.

The three walked rapidly through the castle, out towards the area leading to the tunnels carved into the White Cliffs of Dover. She had no idea where they were going or indeed what they were doing but that was nothing new since war had been declared. Everyone was just following orders and hoping for the best as far as she could see.

Chapter 12

"*You need to withdraw your forces and regroup!*" a loud accented voice was exclaiming when Perry opened a door into a brightly lit room deep inside the tunnels. "They are hunched down on the borders of Holland and Belgium being commanded by men on horseback, digging trenches for God's sake! Despite all of the information men and women have died smuggling to you, you still insist on believing this war will follow the pattern of the last one. *You are imbeciles! Get your people out of there!*"

Krista stared at the men gathered in this huge room. Some were seated around a table that she imagined could have graced a boardroom. Others were standing in small groups around the room. The mixture of uniforms and the predominance of heavy gold braiding on those uniforms was eye-catching. There were Wrens serving refreshments while others were taking notes, she noticed. What on earth was going on and why was she here?

"Hans speaks the truth." Philippe Dumas stepped away from one such group to state.

Krista's eyes almost popped out of her head. What was Philippe doing in a group comprising Rear Admiral Andrews, Captain Waters and the Grey Man?

"We are military men!" a seated older man in the uniform of a Field Marshal barked. "We take our orders from the top – our duty is to carry out those orders."

"*Then you need to get rid of those at the top!*" the first speaker, Hans, shouted.

"You are talking mutiny, man," the field marshal said sadly.

"*I am talking survival!*" Hans fell into the chair behind him.

"We will achieve nothing yelling at each other and pointing fingers." Clarence Brownlow-Hastings stepped forward. "We have gathered here to share information and discuss strategy. It is past time that all of the Nation's services gathered together to discuss what will be needed."

"Permission to speak, admirals." Reggie Andrews had had enough. They were behaving like schoolboys bent over their homework – hiding their work with their bodies – in case someone should try to copy. They were Britain's defence forces. They needed to act as one unit.

"*Granted!*" came from several throats.

"We have here a representation of each arm of our country's defence forces." He pointed to groups around the room. "The Army, Navy and Air forces not to mention the men of the newly formed intelligence branch. If each would share their thoughts and the actions they plan or hope to take, we might be able to achieve something worthwhile here today."

"I will not be a part of a mutiny," the field marshal growled.

"The findings and plans made here today will be carried to Churchill. We need to show our support but we cannot blindly follow men we feel are in error. Our country needs us to protect and serve." Reggie wondered if he was getting through to these men.

"Gentlemen," Clarence Brownlow Hastings felt he was taking the greatest gamble of his career when he introduced himself to the company, "I am acting head of the newly formed intelligence-gathering service and as such I say to you all ..." he looked around the room, being sure to catch the eye of a representative of each service, "that we are in no way prepared to fight Hitler. The man has been planning his offensive for years while we – along with our allies – have rolled over and licked his boots."

He expected roars of outrage. When none came, he continued.

"This man," he gestured towards Hans, "a German, has risked his life and that of his family to bring us much-needed information. This man," he gestured to

Philippe, "is French and he too has brought us vital news. Yet none of you in this room know them. They have strolled amongst you with impunity."

Now he received roars of outrage.

"The women walking around the room serving tea and coffee, being treated like waitresses at the corner Lyon's café, are highly trained women yet none of you noticed them or objected to their presence. Any or all of these people could have killed you and walked away."

"Is there a purpose to this melodrama?" one admiral asked.

"I can see that none of you believe me." Clarence had to convince these men of the danger Britain and the world faced. "Captain Waters … if you would." There was no longer a need for secrecy and he had discussed the matter of calling on Waters with him.

"In the winter of last year," Captain Waters stepped forward to say, "I, with the permission of my commanding officers arranged a sortie into Germany for personal reasons." He ignored the grumbles and mutters that went around the room. "Perry and Krista, if you would step forward." He waited until the pair had come to stand at his shoulders before continuing. "These two travelled into Belgium and crossed the border into Germany. They were tasked with removing my sister from danger and gathering what information they could about the state of Germany and its people."

"Obviously they got in and out with no problem. Is there a point to this?" an Army General asked.

"The point, General, is that we need to listen to

people not in the forces, not in the command structure. We cannot just dismiss them. We need to listen to the people on the ground who hear and see far more than we give them credit for. We need to be aware of the world outside our own little section." Waters wished he could bang a few heads together.

"All of this could be submitted in written reports we could read at our leisure," an admiral groaned.

"There will be few written reports floating around for anyone to get their hands on and read," Clarence Brownlow Hastings growled.

"You!" an army general pointed at Perry. "You are wearing an army uniform with the insignia for special services. What have you to say for yourself?"

"I am Peregrine Fotheringham Carter," Perry stood to attention. "The admiral's son." He noticed the change in attitude towards him. "And suddenly my words have more meaning for most of you. This is exactly the attitude Captain Waters has stated must change. My words have no more meaning because of an accident of birth than every man, woman and child in the United Kingdom. We will all bleed red in this war."

"Very prettily said," someone muttered. "Get on with it."

"I travelled through Belgium into Germany as Captain Waters has told you. I was in company with this woman." He gestured towards Krista. "A French native born to an Englishwoman, who speaks three languages fluently and has seen more of what is happening in Europe than any other in this room I dare say – yet no one has called on her for her views and opinions." He paused to glare around the room. *"Why — because she is female?"*

"This attitude must change." Philippe stepped forward to stand beside Krista.

"I say ..."

"How dare he ..."

"A foreigner telling us ..."

The mutters and outrage almost shook the room.

"You are all sitting here in your pretty dungeon, feeling so superior to those of us sweating and bleeding in the mud and dirt of this war. You," Philippe pointed rudely at the braid decorating the dress uniforms of the men gathered in the room, "look pretty in your uniforms cleaned and pressed by hands you don't even acknowledge. You are fools. Hitler has eyes and ears everywhere yet you strut around like toy soldiers unaware of the danger around you. This, gentlemen, is your call to arms."

"How dare you!"

"Who do you think you are, you jumped-up Frenchman?"

"You cannot speak to us like that."

Chairs were pushed back and men who had too long been working comfortably in their offices, waited on hand and foot by staff, beat the table and expressed their outrage. They didn't have to listen to any of this, by God.

The Wrens in the room moved as a unit to soothe and settle the disgruntled men, urging them back into their seats and stopping just short of stroking their troubled brows.

"Gentlemen!" Rear Admiral Andrews stepped forward as soon as order was restored to the room. He was one step away from court martial but these fools had to be made to see what was in front of them. He watched the Wrens serve tea and coffee around the table and the room. "You are all dead."

The silence in the room was almost painful.

"The women helping restore order in this room have slit the throats of ..." here Reggie pointed to the highest-ranking officers seated at the table, "all of you blustering ..." he bit back the word *fools* but it was difficult, "officers. If you check your neck you will find marks over your jugular vein. You are, all of you, bleeding to death. Today these women held only markers hidden in their sleeves. If they had been hiding razors no one would walk away from this table." He ignored the shouts and roars – watched as the officers – to a man – clicked their fingers at their subordinates, demanding they check their necks. He turned to the men smirking around the room. "The rest of you have fared no better. The coffee and tea you have been slurping is poisoned!"

"There had better be a darn good reason for this melodrama, rear admiral." The field marshal didn't look so sanguine now. His general had indeed found the mark of what would have been a fatal wound on his neck. He did not enjoy being made to look a fool.

"Hitler will not obey the rules of engagement," Clarence Brownlow Hastings stepped forward to say. "The man is no gentleman. He will not observe the rules set out by the Geneva Convention. In order to engage with him we have to understand how he thinks and acts. This melodrama as you have called it," he waved around the room. "was but a demonstration of what we are up against. Hitler's soldiers are shooting unarmed men, women and children – even babes in arms. He is training beautiful women in espionage while we sit here arguing and positioning for the top spot. *We have to work together.* We must all stand together or we will fall."

To be Continued

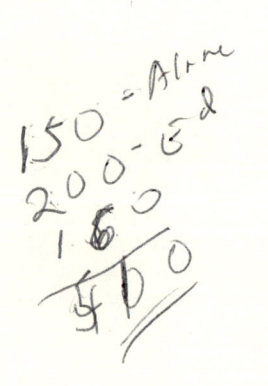

Made in the USA
Middletown, DE
28 July 2025